THE WORST ENEMY

By Steven Havill

THE WORST ENEMY
THE KILLER

THE WORST ENEMY

STEVEN HAVILL

DOUBLEDAY & COMPANY, INC.
GARDEN CITY, NEW YORK
1984

All of the characters in this book
are fictitious, and any resemblance
to actual persons, living or dead,
is purely coincidental.

Library of Congress Cataloging in Publication Data

Havill, Steven.
The worst enemy.

(Double D western)
I. Title.
PS3558.A785W6   1984   813'.54
ISBN: 0-385-18918-4
Library of Congress Catalog Card Number 83–45090
Copyright © 1984 by Steven Havill

1. Fiction - Westerns
2. Westerns - Fiction

For Margaret Havill,
"In memory of her prairie years"
and Kathleen M. Havill,
again, with thanks.

THE WORST ENEMY

se she met me at the door. Her eyes were wide with
ght.

"Mary?" she asked, reaching out.

"Mary's all right, Lucy. She's had a shock." We went
ide. There was a love seat just inside the parlor, and I
t Mary there. She sat with hands clutching the mate-
l of the seat, her eyes searching mine for answers. I
ew Mrs. Kinnon to one side and tried to keep my voice
v and steady. "I think there was a fight in the saloon,
s. Kinnon. A stray bullet hit Becky Servin. I think it
ne out of the saloon and hit her while the two girls
re walking past in the street."

"Oh, my soul . . ."

"Mary's fine. She wasn't struck."

"But Becky?"

"She's dead." I glanced at Mary, then back at her
other. "I'm sorry that I have to leave, but I'm needed.
e child will be all right, I think, but she'll need you
th her. I'll stop by later in the evening to attend her if
u think she needs it."

Mrs. Kinnon nodded, the shock of it all leaving her
echless.

"I'm sorry I have to go," I said again and reached for
e door behind me.

"Of course," Mrs. Kinnon said, and then her full atten-
n was on her daughter. I left quickly and ran back up
e street toward the Apple Core. The street was alive
en, with several people milling about. I saw John
nnerman from the bank two doors down from the
oon, and I grabbed his elbow.

"John, find either Frank Servin or Bea, or both, and get
em to my office. Their daughter's been shot."

"Good God, Robert. How in heaven did that happen?"

CHAPTER 1

Little Becky Servin—eleven years old, golden-haired,
and pug-nosed—died violently in the middle of the afternoon on a hot August day in 1891. Many months later
I could almost bring myself to call it an accident. But
then, in the heat of the moment, I called it murder.

The senselessness of her death so consumed everyone's thoughts, including mine, that four more people
were to die in the following five days—equally senselessly. Had it been wartime, and her death a diversionary
tactic, the incident couldn't have been better planned.
But it wasn't wartime. At least, it wasn't the kind of war
where you knew your enemy from the beginning.

I saw her killed. Thankful that afternoon that I had no
patients to attend, I sat on the small balcony outside my
second-floor living quarters, my office downstairs empty
and quiet. I was perched on the balcony railing, smoking
my pipe, wishing for rain. The sky was a blank blue,
untouched by clouds, with the late summer cottonwoods
beyond and above the edge of town nervously trembling
their leaves in the crackling heat. I was reading a four-
month-old journal when I heard the tinkle of the girls'
voices coming down the street. Becky was walking in the
middle of a favorite gaggle of friends. There was no
traffic in the street, only a horse or two tied at the rail of
the Apple Core Saloon, and the girls walked down the
middle of the street, kicking dust.

I went back to my reading, and only a chorus of especially loud giggles brought my head back up. Two of the
girls had split off from the group, hop-skipping down a
side lane to their home behind the church. Becky Servin
and Mary Kinnon continued on alone, and their giggles
came when they saw me, haunch on railing, pipe chuff-
ing, eyebrows furrowed in concentration.

"Good afternoon, Dr. Patterson!" Mary called, her
voice as clear and crystal as fine glass.

I took the pipe out of my mouth. "And the same, Mary.
You girls learn anything today?"

They didn't answer but dissolved in giggles as only
girls can do, thinking my question uproarious. That's
right, I thought, school hasn't started yet. They waved,
and I grinned, watching them hit every hummock of
dust in the street with their white shoes. They passed in
front of the saloon, and then time sped up. A jagged spur
of wood burst out of the surface of the thin, swinging
door of the saloon. Becky Servin's blond head jerked
sharply to her right, and she took two awkward, dancing
steps that sent her colliding with Mary Kinnon, then fell
in an awkward heap in the dirt. There were noises, coming at the same time, from the saloon, savage thunder-
clap mixed with two sharp, cracking barks. I couldn't
have told you then, or afterward, the order of those
sounds, only that they were there at the same moment
when Becky Servin was flung into the dust of the street.
Mary Kinnon's hands came up to her mouth, and she
backed slowly away from Becky, back toward the side of
the street under my balcony.

I dropped the journal and my pipe and swung over the
rail of my balcony, catching the edge of the railing and
then dropping to catch the edge of the balcony flooring.

My boots hit the dust of the street just beyond t[
walk, and I ran to Becky, still with no real ide[
had happened.

I wasn't long finding out. She was bleeding
from the neck, and it had been the sight of t[
that caused Mary Kinnon, innocent of the visio[
things, to back away, numb with horror. I be[
lifting the thick blond hair away, and then sa[
my haunches. It takes no real skill to recogniz[
struction caused by a bullet, and I had seen n[
my share. And I knew that no skill of mine c[
that child. The slug had clipped her spine as e[
as a child would snap off the downy head of
dandelion.

"Doc, what is it?" someone at my elbow ye[

"She's dead," I said, then looked quickly ov[
Mary Kinnon, a stunned waif of ten with no [
derstanding what she was seeing. I took off m[
covered the dead girl, then stood up, standing[
her body and Mary's wide eyes. "Take her to m[
said, then turned and ran to Mary.

I scooped her up in my arms. She was skin[
bones through the lace and calico, and right th[
care what mayhem had been wrought in the s[
such violence that it had spilled out into the st[
said nothing. She clung to me, her body stiff [
ning to shake. Her home was just down the str[
the Servins', and I walked as quickly as I co[

I was entering the gate, striding up to the
front porch, when Mary said, "Dr. Patterson, [

I put my palm on the top of her head. [
Mary."

Mrs. Kinnon had apparently seen my app[

"I don't know. But get them, will you? And have you seen McCuskar?"

"I think he's in there," Bannerman said, indicating the saloon.

I nodded. "And John . . . the girl's dead. Someone, I don't know who, took her to my office. Don't just let the parents walk in unprepared. I'll be there as soon as I can."

As it turned out, there was not much to detain me at the Apple Core. Marshal Vince McCuskar was in the saloon, all right, and, I found out shortly, had been all along. No one knew exactly what had happened, and everyone had his own version. It didn't really matter. Two men lay dead as stones. The generally accepted version was that Tom Bates, a sometimes hardworking logger, had taken a violent dislike to Ira Becker, a cowpuncher who should have had better things to be doing. Whatever the initial cause of the scuffle, it had ended violently and noisily. Becker had drawn a revolver, and Marshal McCuskar had tried to interfere, holding the scatter-gun that was his habitual companion. In short order Tom Bates had grabbed the shotgun from the marshal's pudgy little hands.

Everyone agreed that Becker had fired first; then the logger, already mortally wounded, had let fly with the shotgun, spreading the cowpuncher all over the front of the bar. It had been one of Becker's wild shots that had gouged through the saloon door and killed little Becky Servin.

I spent thirty seconds determining that there was no need of my services. McCuskar tried to grab my arm, his pale face working furiously, but I shook him off.

"Maybe you'd like to explain to Frank or Bea Servin

just how this mess happened," I said, leaning close to the marshal. I could smell the whiskey on him.

"Now see here," McCuskar started to say.

"See here what?"

He pulled himself up to his full height and hiked up his trousers and gun belt. He nodded at the two corpses and the crowd of the curious. "I'll take care of things here," he said officiously. "You just do what you can for that little girl."

"The little girl is dead, Marshal."

"Oh." McCuskar rubbed a hand over the stubble on his chin. He was a short man, going to fat, with wide-set, dark eyes that never seemed to settle in one spot for very long. "I'm genuinely sorry about that, Doc."

I cursed under my breath and turned on my heel, leaving the Apple Core. It took the rest of the afternoon to clean up the emotional mess that incident caused. Mr. and Mrs. Servin went home to comfort each other and try to figure out what they had done to deserve their fate. Mrs. Kinnon spent the rest of the day, I'm sure, trying to explain the same sorts of things to her daughter. The three bodies, two large and one small, went to Blumenthal's Parlor, to be prepared for the final public showing the next day. I'd heard more than once in the two years I had been a practicing physician in Cooperville that our funeral parlor was one of *the* things that made the town modern. No more laying out in the home. Ruben Blumenthal took care of it all. And so, in short order, the street was back to normal, the Apple Core Saloon patrons had an endless supply of conversation fodder, my office was empty, and Blumenthal's was full.

I straightened things up five or six times, all the while thinking about Vince McCuskar, and finally got so angry that I locked the office and walked over to the bank, hoping to find John Bannerman there. He was, his normally florid face still pale. He waved me into his small office and shut the door behind us.

"Let me get you something," he said and poured a generous glass of brandy, handing it to me before pouring one for himself.

"It shouldn't have happened, John."

Bannerman sipped the brandy, then sat down behind his desk. He was an imposing figure, frocked in black with a narrow string tie on a spotless white shirt. He turned the glass, gazing into the amber liquid.

"No, it shouldn't have. But," and he shrugged. "It did, didn't it?"

"You know that McCuskar was in the saloon all along?" I asked.

"Yes, I know he was."

"If he hadn't been there, whooping it up with all the rest, maybe it wouldn't have happened."

"Maybe not."

"Damn it, John, you can do something about it. You and Hoskings and the others hired McCuskar. You can fire him just as easy."

"And then?"

"And then . . . well, then find someone who can do a marshal's job the way it should be done."

John Bannerman looked over at me, his eyes heavy and weary. "You want the job?"

"Don't be ridiculous."

"All right then. No one else does either." He leaned back. "It's not easy finding a lawman for a little one-horse town, Robert."

"We can do better than McCuskar."

"He certainly has his faults. I admit that."

I laughed dryly. "He's an ignorant drunk, to name but two faults."

Bannerman sighed. "Robert, what can I say? We need someone. Vince McCuskar has managed to do a fairly respectable job, all in all. The council will talk about what happened today, I can assure you of that. But what the solution is . . ." He held up his hands. "Maybe we will let him go, but that won't bring back Becky Servin or the two men in the saloon. I'm as sorry as you are, believe me."

I talked with, or at, Bannerman for nearly another hour, and nothing came of it. I hadn't really expected anything, either, to be honest. When you pay a man twenty dollars a month flat wages, you don't exactly get the pick of the litter. Twenty dollars was all the town council would pay for a marshal, and men like Vince McCuskar were the result.

And so I fumed. I went to the Branding Iron for supper and ordered and then found I didn't have an appetite, shoving the small steak away without so much as a bite. That was the first stroke of good fortune that day, even though I didn't know it at the time. Back at my office I tried to read and couldn't. So I settled for the only intelligent thing to do under the circumstances. I found a bottle of ninety-proof medicine and ordered myself to take several doses. And then several more. I didn't feel any better, but the mind-numbing stupor let me get some sleep.

CHAPTER 2

The next morning broke clear and brilliant, and the damn birds seemed to take distinct pleasure in blathering right outside my window. I rolled over quickly and jammed my head under the pillow and then groaned at the stab of pain that rocked my skull. Hard spirits and I had never gotten along well together, and I lay still for a few minutes, thinking about the half-empty bottle down in my office.

And then I remembered more about the day before, and my indignation began to flare again. If John Bannerman and the rest of the town fathers thought I would let the matter of Vince McCuskar's negligence lie unchallenged, they had another think coming. I turned over on my back and lay that way for a while, one hand over my eyes.

As the town's only physician, wasn't I responsible for the physical well-being of the citizens? Why, certainly. When the town marshal drank it up with the boys in the local saloon, too inebriated to enforce the law before a harmless, bright-eyed, and totally innocent bystander got killed, then it was my responsibility to do something about it.

That's the way I saw it that morning. I was twenty-nine years old, five years out of medical college, three years out of a hitch with the United States Army as a lieutenant in the medical corps. I was indeed the only

physician in the town of Cooperville, my office nearly
one hundred and fifty miles south and east of Denver.

Fueled by my sense of righteousness, I rolled out of
bed, planting my feet firmly on the bare wood floor to
provide some support for a head that felt like it would
spin off into space at any moment.

I waited a moment, then struggled my lanky frame
upright and lunged across the room, catching the edge
of the old bureau with both hands. I sighed and looked at
myself in the small chip of a mirror and grimaced.

Fifteen minutes later, when I stumbled downstairs
into the dim morning light of my office, I was mildly
surprised to find I was not alone in my own house. A man
I thought I recognized as one of the mill workers from
the cooperage was seated in one of the two chairs that
marked my waiting room. He shouldn't have been there.
I had things to do. I wanted McCuskar's scalp right then.
I didn't need any other patients. I was something less
than my usual sunny self.

"Mornin', Doc," the man said quietly. Now I usually
pride myself in beginning my diagnosis from the first
time I lay eyes on a patient and from the first time I hear
his voice. Illness lurks in the emotion as well as the body,
I had once heard a professor say, and I had always believed that. But other things were in my head just then.

"Uh," I said in reply and ran a hand through my thick
hair. "The door wasn't locked?"

"No, it weren't."

"Well, then come on in." He already was in but got up
slowly and moved obediently to a solitary straight-back
chair that I used for examinations. He stood, seeming
uncertain, and I waved a hand impatiently. "Sit down, sit
down." He did so gratefully. "What can I do for you?"

He was a strong man, nearly six feet in height and built solidly, with a shock of sandy hair that fell over his forehead and a wide, pleasant face.

"I'm feelin' poorly, Doc."

"So I would assume, or you wouldn't be here."

There was an uncomfortable silence, and then I took his wrist, pulling out my watch with my other hand, snapping open the gold case. I stood silently and had to count twice to make sure, not because of anything unusual but because my mind refused to focus on the problems at hand.

I clicked the watch shut and stood back, looking at the man. "So tell me about it."

The man shrugged slightly. "My head feels like it might be about to bust wide open," he said, and I saw him wince even as he spoke. That explained why he was speaking so quietly. I had some sympathy for his condition.

"And?"

"I can't eat nothin', and I got the trots like won't quit."

"Drinking last night?"

"No more'n usual."

"And how much is that?"

"Couple a pints, maybe."

"Bother you then?"

"Yep. I unloaded right fast."

"You eat yesterday?"

"Couldn't."

"Then the day before?"

"Felt fine then."

"Huh. No trouble breathing?"

"No."

I reached over and rested the flat of my hand on his

forehead. "Huh," I said again. "Didn't feel anything coming on?"

"No."

"Joints hurt?"

"Sure as hell do."

"Huh. Well, sure sounds like you got yourself one fast-paced sample of the grippe." I ran a hand through my hair again and stepped back half a pace when the man coughed violently.

"Damn, that hurts," he said and looked up at me through misty eyes.

"Chest hurt when you cough?"

"No, my head."

"Oh. Well, sir, I'd suggest you find yourself a bed and take to it for a spell, until you feel just a little better."

"You ain't got nothin' you can give me?"

"Well, I guess I do, for that headache, anyway. Bed's the best thing." I went to my pharmaceutical cabinet, took one of the small paper envelopes, and carefully dipped a few grains of well-cut opiate out of a bottle, transferring the powder carefully to the envelope. I handed the envelope to the man. "Mix that in a glass of water. Use about a quarter of what's there each time. And get yourself some sleep."

The man took the envelope and nodded carefully, as if afraid his head would fall off. He grinned sheepishly. "I guess I best be off to find a privy again," he said.

"Let me know if you don't feel better," I said.

I watched him hobble out, fragile but in a hurry nevertheless before he soiled himself in public. It didn't occur to me then, but I hadn't even asked him his name.

My watch came out of my pocket again, and I looked at the time. It should be possible to take someone's pulse and at the same time make note of the time, but I had never been able to do that. It was nearly eight, and John Bannerman would be in his bank and would have had enough time to think about matters of grave concern— his town marshal for one. My dislike for Vince McCuskar was not based on the Servin girl's death alone. I considered him a heavy-handed, ignorant slob, always had since the first day that I met him. Watching him stand on the boardwalk six months before, grinning from ear to ear while a trail-dusted band of drovers pushed a herd of cattle right down the main street, had not helped my opinion of him any. I had been taking out a pair of very infected tonsils at the time, and the dust had almost choked both me and my patient. A little investigation had informed me that driving cattle through the town was a local custom of sorts. It took me only a week to gain assurances that the ludicrous custom would stop, but through no effort on McCuskar's part. It had taken my threat to move my practice elsewhere, leaving the town to fend for itself with a winter coming. The merchants had said the show of cattle strength was good for business. I countered and said it was the most inexcusable threat to general health I had ever seen. I won. I hadn't seen a cow on the main street of Cooperville for more than six months. McCuskar had no liking for his job of enforcing the new ordinance, but John Bannerman sided with me and threatened to fire the lawman.

My plan was then clear, at least to me. If McCuskar wouldn't stay out of the saloon, and stay away from strong drink while on duty, as any policeman should, then he would have to go. A triple funeral was proof enough that I was right. Had I known right then that problems involving Vince McCuskar were so insignificant, so minor, compared with what was ahead, my plans would have been different. So I straightened my string tie, brushed off my coat, and left the empty office, heading through the bright light of morning and self-righteousness to John Bannerman's office.

I didn't make it. John Bannerman, imposing as always, met me in the street not far from the cottonwood-bordered lane that led back to his sturdy brick home.

"Robert, can you come inside please?" His tone was urgent and his face pale.

I was squinting against the morning sun as it thumped on my sore head, and I had been busy rehearsing my speech that I planned to deliver to this friendly banker. But even my eyes, fighting the internal banging of my system, could see that John Bannerman was in a bad way. He was worried, and for him that was unusual.

I fell in step with him without question and blessed the deep shade of those trees that lined his walk. He didn't say anything else until we were almost at the front steps.

"Janey's awful sick, Robert. I'd like you to take a look at her if you have the time."

"I have the time," I said. "I was just coming to see you."

Bannerman didn't comment on that but instead led me inside the house. It was a familiar home to me. I had been the beneficiary of several of Jane Bannerman's dinners, particularly when she started feeling sorry for me on holidays, with no family nearby. The home was a quiet statement of John Bannerman's success as a banker —comfortable, a little too dark for my tastes, but with an ambience normally not found in homes that dotted small towns the likes of Cooperville.

"She's in the master bedroom upstairs," the banker

said, and he took the stairs two at a time. I followed, remembering for the first time that I did not have my black medical bag with me.

The bedroom was dark, with no breath of air stirring. Some folks still believed that the infirm should be further tortured by withholding fresh air and sunshine. I halted in the doorway, letting John go to his wife's bedside first.

"Robert's here," he said quietly and then beckoned me over.

"Open the curtains, for Pete's sake," I said not altogether civilly. "It's dark as a tomb in here." He did so, and the sunlight, dappled by the jumping cottonwood leaves outside the window, sparkled into the room. We all winced from the sudden light, me most of all.

There was no doubt Jane Bannerman was ill. She was no hypochondriac, a disease that frequented lonely women of the small, frontier towns, ladies with nothing on their hands but time and hard work. Indeed, she was one of the most solid women I had ever met, both physically and mentally.

She looked up at me with brown eyes that were glazed, and deep lines were in her forehead from the pain.

"Head hurt?" I asked, placing a hand on her forehead gently.

"Something frightful, Doctor," she said.

I counted her pulse and found nothing unusual there except a slight elevation that I would have expected with any serious illness. While I was counting, my lips moving with each number, I noticed her pillowcase. The normally spotless linen was stained in one or two places with dried blood.

"You've been bleeding, Jane?"

She moved a hand listlessly. "I haven't had a nosebleed since I was a child. Now that's all I seem to do," she said and smiled weakly.

"Nauseous?"

"Frightful," she answered and looked over at John, who stood at the foot of the bed. "I'm afraid if John has to empty the bedpan once more, he'll take me out in the mountains and leave me."

"I doubt that," I said and sat down on the edge of her bed. The edges of her lips were showing a slight bluish tinge, and I was surprised, but there wasn't enough cyanosis there to ring any alarm bells in my head. My head was having enough troubles of its own.

"Have you tried sitting up much?"

"Heavens no," she answered and shook her head slightly. "I get so dizzy I'm afraid I'd fall on my face."

"Anything else you can tell me?"

"Well . . . I . . ." and she stopped, flushing slightly.

"I am a physician, Jane. Now's not the time to be delicate."

"Well . . . my . . . my stool has been bloody since early this morning." She seemed relieved to have that shameful sentence over with.

"Really?" I said again with mild surprise. I gazed at her, swathed in the linen and nightgown right up to the chin. I saw her hand move under the linen, move in a tentative scratch, and that brought another question to mind.

"Any eruptions of any kind, anywhere?"

"Well . . ."

"Out with it, Jane."

"Well . . . I have a . . . carbuncle . . . at least one."

"Do I get to see this frightful thing, or do I have to just guess?"

"Well . . . there's one on my back, just below the nape of my neck, that bothers me some. It came yesterday."

She started to lean upward, and I quickly moved to help her. Sure enough, there was a carbuncle, with its dark center ugly and the inflammation spreading outward.

"Yes, you certainly do," I said and helped her rearrange herself on the bed. "I guess we can take care of that all right." I stood up and turned to John. "I left my medical bag over in my office, John. She will rest easy until I can come back." I looked back down at her. "You're a sick young lady," I said, "and you're in the best possible place. I'd say you have one nasty case of intestinal grippe. I'll get something to ease the headache and something for that boil. Don't scratch at it or disturb it in any way. We don't want an infection there."

I turned to her husband. "And you might open one of those windows and let some fresh air in here. That would make her feel better straightaway."

Bannerman followed me downstairs and out into the warm, bright morning.

"She'll be all right?"

I grunted. "Hell, yes, John, she'll be all right. Nothing for you to worry about."

He looked relieved. "What was it you wanted to see me about earlier?"

I rubbed my forehead, beginning to feel almost human for the first time that morning. "Ah yes. I was going to give you a sermon on Vince McCuskar."

Bannerman smiled. "That again."

"I'm serious, John. That man has to go. I'm surprised the folks didn't string him up yesterday."

"No one blamed him for what happened."

"You don't think they should have?"

"I don't know what to think except that what happened was a regrettable accident."

"I'm sure that will make the Servins feel better at the funeral this afternoon."

John Bannerman looked at me, his eyes assessing. "You're really serious about all this, aren't you?"

I laughed shortly. "Hell, yes, I'm serious. Shouldn't I be? I'm surprised everyone else is taking it so lightly."

"Lightly is the wrong word, Robert."

"Then instruct me. Should McCuskar have been in the saloon in the middle of the afternoon, egging those two birds on until they killed themselves and a little girl, too? Should he have been so drunk that he allowed another man to take his gun away from him and use it?"

"Of course not, Robert."

"Well, then?"

"Well . . . what do you expect from us?"

"Fire the son of a bitch is what I expect. John, just tell me why that's so difficult?"

Bannerman sighed. "This isn't Chicago, Robert. We don't have a whole list of recruits to draw from."

"There's bound to be someone else. I don't see much in the way of Vince McCuskar's character that's so hard to replace."

The banker held up both hands. "We'll talk about it at the next council meeting. That's the only promise I can make. I agree with you. But let's not be hasty. Maybe McCuskar learned his lesson. He's been of some value up to now."

"When's the next meeting?"

"We haven't set the time."

"Let me know when you do, would you?"

"Certainly. Although, to be honest, right now I'm more concerned about my wife than about our town marshal."

I took the gentle hint and patted Bannerman on the shoulder. "I'll get my bag."

It took me only a few moments to prepare medications and gather my instruments, and by the time I left my office I thought my mind was beginning to function somewhere close to normal. I was still preoccupied and shouldn't have been.

I returned to the Bannermans' and worked for nearly an hour, taking care of the carbuncle and medicating the powerful grippe that was making the woman so uncomfortable. When I left, Jane Bannerman seemed to be resting comfortably.

For the next several hours I was busy with my practice, seeing a bad tooth that I pulled, a shattered leg that I tried to set as best I could, and an infection in the side of a horse's neck that I cleaned and disinfected. Toward noon I thought I pretty much had the town's ills under control. Only one man remained in my office. He had waited patiently, maybe seeming a little ill at ease with the confines of my small office. There was a liberal coating of dust on his clothes, and his chaps were wide and fringed. I ignored the big revolver that he wore on his hip. I was more interested in the way he seemed to blend in with the woodwork, hardly moving a muscle while he waited.

"And what can I do for you?"

"Name's Jensen."

"Well, Mr. Jensen?" I asked. He didn't look ill, just uninterested.

"Two buddies a mine are sick."

"Well, where are they?"

"Out to trail camp."

I groaned to myself. "Where's that?"

"Bout five mile north a here."

"Can they come in?"

The man shook his head. "I told 'em they should, but they wouldn't. Now they's so sick they can hardly move. One of 'em keeps bouncin' around like he's got the dance."

I didn't quite know what that meant and said so.

"Keeps flopping in his bedroll like a dog with a broke back."

That made a little more sense. "You mean he's got convulsions?"

"Yep, I guess that's what I mean."

"They been sick long?"

Jensen shook his head. "Was fine up to yesterday, round about noon or shortly thereafter. Hit 'em both hard. Squirtin' from both ends. Christ almighty, Ben's even bleedin' some from the face."

"From the face?"

"Nose," Jensen said, pointing at his own like maybe I wouldn't know about that piece of anatomy, "and ears, even," and he tugged at his own.

"Bloody stool?"

"Bloody what?"

"Stool." I would have pointed to make myself clear but didn't see any polite way of doing so.

"What the hell's stool, anyways?"

"Shit," I said pleasantly. "Does either of them have blood in their shit?"

"Oh," Jensen said. "That. How the hell should I know that? I ain't exactly looked."

I grinned. "Maybe someone should exactly look," I said.

"I was hopin' you could come on out. We can pay you."

"That's always pleasant news," I said, trying to sound cheerful but not feeling the least bit enthusiastic about riding a horse with my head so loosely mounted to my neck. "Your luck would have it that you've hit a thin spot in my otherwise packed practice." Jensen didn't grin or chuckle or laugh at my attempt at humor but simply stood, waiting for me to put my things together. I did so and walked quickly over toward the livery. Jensen followed on his own dappled gray, keeping a respectful ten paces behind.

"Mornin', Doc," Earl Baines, the livery boy, called. He helped me with the heavy saddle, help that wasn't really necessary, since I wasn't even close to being an invalid in any way but in my head. Saddled and bridled, Clara allowed herself to be led out into the street, a mouthful of hay still being processed.

"Lead on," I said, and Jensen wheeled his mount and made off down the street. Clara's eyes got bright at the prospect of a chase, and she made after the gray, tail flowing straight out, mane bouncing with each stride. I realized I had forgotten my hat, but the sun felt good on my head, the warmth seeping down through my scalp like a hot balm.

Jensen was pulling away a little, and I booted Clara gently in the ribs. She responded with an uncollected lunge that said, "My goodness, can we really?" and then she was in a full, ground-eating gallop, keeping pace effortlessly with Jensen's gray.

CHAPTER 3

The camp had all the earmarks of a temporary resting spot gone out of control. Whatever attempts at neat camp-keeping there may have been were obviously forgotten. The small glade, deep in the shadows of a dense grove of juniper, was littered with refuse. A discarded can of KG baking powder, twenty-five ounces for twenty-five cents on the lid, rolled away as the front hoof of Jensen's gray touched it. A small blackened coffeepot sat off to one side of the fire, both untended and cold.

I saw two other horses tethered some yards away, but all the tack was close to the ashes of the fire, and the two men lay a yard apart, one of them partially covered by a blanket, the other on top of his bedroll.

I let Clara go off by herself, and she seemed a little miffed at the lack of forage.

The condition of the two men quickly set my mind to medical matters. I had no sooner squatted down by the first of the two patients than he looked at me, wildly, I thought, and went into seizure. The convulsion didn't last long, and the man quickly subsided into an exhausted stupor. I saw out of the corner of my eye that Jensen was off with the horses, uncomfortable with the notion of illness. I concentrated on my patients. The man I saw first, the one who had been on top of his bedroll and convulsing, was now quiet, lips bluish, and breathing with difficulty. I listened to his chest, and the rales were loud and harsh.

"How the hell can you get pneumonia in weather like this?" I asked aloud, but the man was beyond answering. I listened some more and didn't like the sound of his heart, laboring and the beat ragged. I stripped off his dirty shirt, receiving no help at all—it was like undressing a sack of grain—and then the dirty flannel underwear. "What do we have here?" I said to myself, looking closely at the angry papules on his arms and torso.

I sat back on my haunches and ran my hand through my hair, thinking. A faint trickle of blood ran down from the man's nose. He groaned.

The second cowpuncher, so tall that his knees stuck out below his blanket, was in no better shape. His breathing was so rasping that I didn't even need to use the stethoscope. This one was conscious.

"How long you boys been out here?" I asked him, and he turned watery-gray eyes on me, obviously wondering who I was.

"Christ," he breathed and turned away, doubling up to vomit where he lay. The spew was bloody, and he made matters worse by lapsing into a coughing fit, his face gone pale and then cyanotic. I pulled at the blanket, but he resisted, not out of conscious effort but just fighting any motion that might add to his agony. One long, bony arm came out, and I saw the two papules just above his wrist.

"Jensen," I called. "How long you men been out here?"

There was no answer for a moment, then his quiet voice came from over by the horses. "A spell."

"Terrific. Just how long is that?"

There was no answer, and I looked around. He was feeding his own mount, several yards away from the other two. "How long?" I shouted.

"Couple, three days."

I stood up. "This come on sudden?"

Again there was no answer. Jensen was not a wealth of information. But at least he wasn't sick. I messed with my hair again and strolled over to where he stood with his horse.

"You know, there's no law against coming into town when you get sick."

"I came to town."

"I mean those two," I said, nodding at his partners. "They're so sick now the trip's going to do them no good at all. Maybe they shouldn't even be moved."

"You do what you can, Doc. Here." He reached into his pocket and then stuck out a closed fist. The twenty-dollar piece dropped into my hand.

"You might want to wait and see if I can do them any good," I said, but Jensen just shook his head.

"You know anything about doctorin' horses?" he asked just as I was turning away, back toward the two men.

"Horses? Some. They aren't so different from people."

Jensen jerked a thumb at the two animals that were hobbled. "One of them's sick, too."

When he said that, it was as if a bell, sharp and loud and dangerous, went off in my head.

"Both?" I asked, taking a step toward the animals.

"Just the bay."

"Move your animal and the other one over to the other side of the clearing," I said quickly, not knowing why. It just seemed like a natural thing to do. I looked quickly over at Clara, but she was some distance away, also on the far side of the clearing.

I walked over toward the bay and saw at once that he was standing with his head down, not eating, and eyes nearly closed. He did not lift his head at my approach and didn't budge a leg. I ran a hand down his flank, and he felt hot, and just above the stifle was a swelling that was both deeply inflamed and obviously tender, because the bay took a flinching, listless sidestep at my touch. I lifted the horse's lip and saw that the gums were a deep reddish-blue.

"Sorry, old friend," I said to the animal, "but I've got human patients who come first." I turned and saw that Jensen had moved the other horses, and he was lashing his own bedroll behind his saddle, all neat and tightly tucked. I didn't think anything of that. It seemed natural enough. Anyone who spent another night in that camp without the need was crazy. His next action I hadn't expected. With a last glance around the camp, he swung up on his mount, gathered the reins of the other horse, and spurred away.

"Hey, there," I called after him. He pulled his horse up short and twisted in the saddle, face impassive. "I might need a hand with these two," I said, nodding at the men.

"Thanks for comin', Doc," Jensen said, and then he turned and rode off, leaving me and my horse with two sick men and another dying animal.

"Hey!" I shouted again, but to no effect. Jensen was gone. I cursed. "Real sense of loyalty," I muttered.

The first cowboy I had examined was unconscious, breathing with great difficulty. The lanky one, still clutching his blanket up under his chin, seemed a little better off, but not much. Using a bottle of strong carbolic acid, I first rinsed my hands, being careful to work the strong disinfectant under my nails and between my fingers. Then I stood for a long moment, hands evaporating dry, thinking hard and wondering what I should do. Part of my problem was solved in the next few minutes. The first man convulsed again and then lapsed back with a small groan into a fit of labored breathing. Strong suspicions about what was plaguing the two men were forming in my mind, and because they were weakening so rapidly, I decided on pretty liberal doses of brandy as a restorative. I had the brandy out and just about to the lips of the man I had seen first when his breathing hesitated, gasped, hesitated again, and then stopped. I tried for a pulse and found none. His eyes had rolled up, just the whites showing through the half-open lids.

I knew of few infectious diseases that killed so quickly and brutally. In this case, a strong man, a young man hardened, it seemed, by years on the range and in perfect health, was dead inside of just a few days. The clues that led to my diagnosis were meshing into a pattern, enough so that I was sure of what had hit the camp. I apparently wasn't alone in knowing.

I turned my head to look at the tall, rangy man who lay next to the corpse and found that he was watching me. He had twisted around in the blankets so that he lay on his left side, and he was having a good deal of difficulty with his breathing. His eyes were almost clear, though, and I assumed that he could understand me. I pulled a corner of the blanket over the dead man's face and stood up. The second cowboy spoke before I had a chance.

"Dead, ain't he?" he asked.

"Yes," I said. "There wasn't much I could do." I said that without realizing the statement could apply to ei-

If he had planned to answer that, the sickness interfered, because the convulsions, savage and abrupt, hit him. His spine arched so that he lifted nearly a foot, and his head slammed the ground so hard I thought it would knock him senseless. For the next ten minutes or so I was pretty busy and managed to get some morphine into him —a stronger dose than I would have liked.

When he had quieted down some, I pulled the blanket off and made a more thorough examination. The papules were present in sinister abundance, and the last convulsion had set off free hemorrhaging from his nose and mouth. For a moment it seemed like he was again lucid, and there was much I needed to know.

"This Brown," I said. "He was the man that came in for me?"

Jensen managed a nod, but his time was more taken up with the task of breathing, and it was more difficult for him by the minute. There was nothing for me to do but wait. It must have been a clot, breaking loose from his ravaged lungs, that killed him, because when he died less than an hour later, just as the sun touched the tops of the junipers surrounding the camp, he went quietly. Just some half-hearted grabbing for breath, and then he was gone.

I had no way to bury the bodies, and the last thing I wanted was to bring them back into town with me. I shucked my coat, rolled up my sleeves, and set to work. There was a profusion of dead wood around the camp, and I built a roaring fire in the pit the cowpunchers had dug for their cooking. Into the fire went the bedding, most of the clothing, even the leather gun belts and holsters. I stuck the two revolvers into my black bag. That left me with two corpses in their underwear. After

ther cowpuncher. But the man who was still alive realized it.

"I'd ask a favor," he said thickly and slowly and with
enormous effort.

"I'll do what I can."

"Name's Jensen," he said. "Family line is down"—he
coughed and rasped a deep breath—"down in Santa Fe."
He paused again, collecting his strength. "Kinda wish
you'd get word to 'em."

"That was kin of yours who rode out just now?"

He looked at me, puzzled. "Kin?"

"The man who was with you two. He came to town to
fetch me. He was kin of yours?"

The man almost managed a smile. "He said he was
that?"

"No," I said. "But he called himself by the same name.
Introduced himself as Mr. Jensen."

"That bastard," he said, and he managed a weak grin.
"One good thing he's ever did in his whole life." He
winced. "You watch out for him. There ain't no
tellin' . . ." and he doubled up in such a fit of combined
coughing and vomiting that I thought I would lose him
then and there. When he relaxed momentarily, I knelt
down close by and made to take his pulse, but he jerked
his hand away. The other arm was still buried under the
blanket.

"Leave me be," he said. "There ain't nothin' for it."

"Let me give you some morphine, then," I said. "It
will help with the pain some. You'll rest easy."

"Damn cattle," he said, ignoring me. He closed his
eyes. "I knew they was sick," he muttered, "but Brown
said it didn't make no never mind."

"What cattle?"

a few moments of scouting the area, I found a deep depression where a large juniper had upended and with some sweat pulled the two bodies there, covering them with dirt that I shoveled awkwardly with their own coffeepot. On top of the dirt I piled all the rocks I could find, building a heavy barrow over the remains, enough so that, I hoped, the scavenging animals might be frustrated. The makeshift grave wasn't as deep as I would have liked, but the area was flat ground, with little danger of groundwater running off into a stream or gully. The contagion might stay virulent in the soil, but it wouldn't go far.

When I was finished, I washed my hands and arms thoroughly with carbolic acid. I took a large hypodermic syringe from my bag and walked slowly over to the horse, the sick animal that still stood, quiet as a stone carving, in the trees on the far side of the clearing. The horse didn't move a muscle when I slapped the needle into its neck, didn't even shake its head at the gathering of flies around its eyes and mouth. I withdrew a full syringe of blood and then carefully wrapped the instrument in a roll of cotton before placing it on top of the other hardware in the black medical bag. I hoped the blood would keep sufficiently until I was able to return to Cooperville.

That finished, I pulled the Winchester rifle from the saddle boot that always rode with me and Clara and returned to the sick horse. I took his bridle and led him off to the thickest part of the juniper stand, where I was sure no range cattle would bother to forage. I held the muzzle of the rifle just under his right ear, and when I fired, the animal sank to its knees and then rolled on its side. It was nearly dark, but I took the time to pull more brush over the dead horse. I don't know why. Any scavenger would have been able to worm his way through the limbwood to the carcass. It just seemed the thing to do.

The blood in the syringe would tell me for sure, but at that point there was little question in my mind. Anthrax had killed both cowboys and sickened the horse. How Brown had escaped infection, I didn't know. But I wasn't looking forward to the next few days in Cooperville. However it had happened, I knew then that Jane Bannerman had the disease too. The symptoms, while not as full-blown yet, were the same. The same as the mill worker I had seen early that morning in my office, when my mind was too fuzzed to think straight.

As I walked back toward Clara, where she stood nuzzling the juniper sprigs for want of any better feed, I tried to compose in my mind what I would have to tell John Bannerman. Unless there was a miracle, his middle-aged wife would be dead before another forty-eight hours had passed.

The agony that thought prompted was enough, that I didn't think much about the man Brown and what he might have done to bring that savage disease down on the heads of others. That he could be ruthless was then obvious, leaving his partners to die in agony. What I didn't know then was that it didn't matter much to Brown how he killed, or when. And I didn't know that it was just a quirk, maybe brought on by the sunshine, maybe brought on by nothing at all, that had prompted Brown to seek me out.

CHAPTER 4

I arrived back in Cooperville just after eight o'clock and hadn't dismounted in front of the livery when Earl Baines trotted out and latched onto the bridle of my horse. He looked concerned.

"Mr. Bannerman asks that you come by his house just as soon as you can, Dr. Patterson," he said. I nodded.

"Take Clara for me, will you?" Baines did so, and only as I was striding away did I have an ugly afterthought. I stopped and turned.

"Earl."

"Yes, sir?"

"Keep her separated from any of the other stock, will you?"

"Why's that?"

"Just do it, if you would."

He shrugged. "I'll rub her down and put her in the back stall. Ain't bein' used."

"Fine. But don't bother with the rubdown. Just put her away."

Earl frowned at that, and I could see he was hesitating.

"No rubdown, Earl. I mean it. Just leave her be."

Baines shrugged. "Just as you say," he muttered, shook his head, and led Clara inside. I hadn't seen Clara ground-grazing and doubted that she could have picked up the anthrax bacilli in the camp, but I didn't want to take any chances. Better she was quarantined and

Baines unhappy with me for neglect. I didn't want to take the time to explain all that to him but trusted him to follow my instructions without argument.

Black bag gripped tightly, I made my way as quickly as I could to my own home and office, entering and locking the door behind me. I tossed my coat in a heap in the corner and set the bag on the counter, carefully taking out the cotton-wrapped syringe. It had been more than an hour since I had pulled the blood from the stricken horse, and I hoped that in something less than ten minutes I would have some definite answers. I had made my share of mistakes, for one reason or another, that day, and now I wanted to be sure. But the thing I feared the most was that two dead men and a dead horse said I already knew the answer.

From the closet beside my examining table I took out a tall, slender cherry-wood case and set it with tender care on a small table that faced a curtained window. The wooden case opened down the middle, and I slipped the microscope out, placing the case on the floor. Throughout my travels, first from Chicago to St. Louis, then the years in the Army, and finally to Cooperville, I had guarded that cherry case and its contents as if they were my life.

My father, a moderately well-to-do businessman in Chicago, had asked me what I had wanted upon my graduation from medical school, and my reply had been prompt and, I think, surprised him with its expense.

I lighted a kerosene lamp and placed it on the table so that the microscope's mirror caught the light, passing it up through the diaphragm and into the objectives. I buffed a glass slide on my shirt and then placed a single drop of aniline dye on the glass, holding the slide dead-level. Next I added a scant drop of the blood from the syringe, making a thin smear on the slide.

Once under the power of the microscope, the slide showed all the glorious complexities of blood, including a bacillus that shouldn't have been there. At least, I found myself trying to wish it away. But there could be no mistake. For more than thirty-five years, after the work of Pollender and Brauell, the anthrax bacilli had been widely known and observed. I had seen their sinister little shapes more than a dozen times in medical college coursework and like a host of other students had found myself wondering if I would ever see the bacilli on their own terms, not in the shelter and comfort and, most important, the relative safety of the controlled laboratory.

The bacilli were thick in the blood smear, motionless rods of elongated, jointed cells. The red blood cells, those small, doughnut-shaped miracles of gas transport in the blood, looked fragile and defenseless next to the long threads of the anthrax, each bacillus thread two or three, some as many as ten, times the length of the healthy blood cells.

I moved the slide and carefully surveyed the entire drop, hoping that somehow the bacilli would simply disappear before my eyes. They didn't.

As a last measure, I rose and took down from the shelf above the table my copy of Whittaker's text, leafing quickly through until my fingers stopped the pages at Figure 31, with the caption *"Bacillus anthracis."* I snapped the book shut and slammed it back on the shelf, feeling no need to look in the microscope again for confirmation. I had not been mistaken.

I sloshed a liberal amount of carbolic acid into a pan

and emptied the syringe into the acid, then unscrewed the needle and put the syringe body, needle, and microscope slide into the pan as well.

"There, you little bastards," I said, "cook for a while in that!" It was a small triumph, because there was no way to immerse Jane Bannerman, or the man from the cooperage, in a pan of carbolic acid to kill the anthrax that was infecting them.

I washed my hands again and then put the microscope away, putting off the dreaded visit to the Bannermans'. I didn't know what to do for the woman, and I didn't know what to say to John Bannerman. As if looking for comfort, I opened the Whittaker text again, ignoring the watercolor plate this time, and scanned down through the text for some word of help.

The prognosis for external anthrax, where the bacilli were confined to the skin only, was grave indeed. But for internal anthrax, where the bacilli attacked the lungs, the blood, the gut, grave was hardly the word. I read the unmercifully short paragraph under prognosis:

"Intestinal and thoracic anthrax, being recognized only after general infection, have always, at least at present, a fatal prognosis."

Just like that. Even if Jane Bannerman's heart was still ticking in her bedroom across the village, in her bedroom bowered by the gayly ignorant cottonwoods, she was still a dead woman.

"Get yourself moving," I said aloud, and I dropped Whittaker's tome on the table with a loud whap. With medical bag in hand, and without my coat, I walked down the street to the lane that led to the Bannerman home. My step was heavy. I had never felt so defeated, so utterly, so totally helpless.

John Bannerman, big, dark, grave of visage, greeted me at the door. He managed a thin smile.

"I was beginning to wonder where you were," he said, trying for a more jolly mood than he felt.

"John, let's go inside. To the parlor. I need to talk to you."

He took one close look at the set of my face and took me by the arm. "Of course," he said and ushered me inside. I tossed my bag on a chair and flopped down in another.

"You look like you could use a drink," Bannerman said and didn't wait for an answer. He poured me a stiff brandy and then one for himself.

"How is Jane?" I asked.

Bannerman took a drink of the brandy. If I had been him, that moment, I would have dragged the doctor up the stairs, at gunpoint if necessary. But John Bannerman didn't do that. He waited, trusting me.

"She's terribly weak, Robert," he said simply.

I nodded and then sighed, taking a sip of the brandy. "John, you're a strong man. You're a good friend. I wish there was some way to make all this easier on you, but I can't. I can't think of a way, for the life of me. So if I'm too blunt, too frank, I ask your forgiveness now."

Bannerman sat down, holding his glass between his knees. I think, at that moment, he knew what I was going to say. He was an intelligent man, and he knew that his wife was dying.

"Get on with it, Doctor," he said quietly.

"I was just called out to a camp. A line camp, I think. I buried two cowboys, John. They died of anthrax."

Bannerman looked up at me sharply. "Anthrax?"

"Yes. I'm sure of it."

"I suppose it's too much to ask that you're joking with me." He didn't mean that, but it was all he could think to say . . . something to fill the silence.

"I brought back a blood sample from one of their horses. It's anthrax. No doubt whatsoever."

"Where were they?"

"About five miles from town, out toward the Staples place. North and east."

Bannerman nodded and then made the connection. His face drained of color, and he sat upright. "Jane?"

I nodded.

"My God."

I leaned forward. "John, I'm going to do all I can, but I want you to know, right now, that there's little hope. And forgive me for saying this, but you have an added burden."

John Bannerman just looked at me, his mind not focused on me but on his wife upstairs.

"John," I persisted, "yesterday morning I saw another man. He came to my office. Now I know that he was infected too. I didn't know at the time. I was so goddamned sorry for myself with a hangover and my concern for what happened to the Servin girl that I wasn't thinking straight. If I don't miss my guess, that man is close to death by now. I didn't get his name, but I can find out fast enough. Here's what I want from you."

Bannerman took a long drink of the brandy. "My God," he said again and shook his head. There were tears in his eyes. "What do you need?" There was agony on his face, but his voice was firm, the stolid banker under control.

"We've got to find out where the anthrax contagion came from. There is a connection between those cowpunchers I saw this morning and the infection here in town. Before he died, one of the men mentioned something about cattle and that his sidekick, a fellow named Brown, knew the cattle were sick. Somehow there has to be a connection between that and Jane's illness, as well as the other man from the cooperage. You have to find out what that connection is, John. We have to know, and fast. Otherwise this town will come apart."

"Christ," Bannerman said dully. He looked at me again. "What do I do?"

"I'm going upstairs to be with Jane and do whatever I can. I want you to think, John. What did you and your wife do in the past few days. I want a list. Write it down. We'll go back, step by step, and find out where it all starts."

"Christ," he said again and wiped a hand across his forehead. "I can't even think."

I stood up and picked up the medical bag. It was dead useless weight.

"Try, John. I know you want to be with Jane. But time is critical. If there's any change upstairs, any reason for . . . well, I'll let you know." I left him sitting there and went upstairs.

Jane Bannerman was weak. At first I had entertained thoughts of trying to purge her system with a powerful emetic, since the anthrax was obviously in her gut, but too much time had passed. Perhaps an hour or so after infection the purge might have done some measurable good, but not now, not after at least two days.

With that avenue no longer open to me, I set about systematically treating the external carbuncles, now five in number, and I gave her a dose of five drops of carbolic acid. I listened to her laboring heart, and all the while she watched my face, without saying a word. In an effort to bolster what I knew to be congestive heart failure, I tried alcohol as a stimulant, remembering Whittaker's admonition that "saturation of the blood" with alcohol might be of use. As she struggled to swallow the raw whiskey, I cradled her head. She managed a fraction of an ounce, and I encouraged her to take more.

"As much as you can, dear," I said, trying to make my tone light. "We'll make you so slaphappy you'll be better in no time, except for the hangover."

She smiled wanly, and I placed her head back down on the pillow.

"Is John downstairs?" she asked, her voice no more than a whisper.

"Yes."

"He's such a good man," she said and then lapsed into merciful unconsciousness. Those were the last words she ever said.

During the next hour, the hour before she died, she seemed to be resting peacefully, as if her system had just given up, letting the anthrax run its deadly course. There was nothing else I could do for her, and I went downstairs to tell her husband that he should spend the next few moments with her.

"I have the list," John Bannerman said when I walked into the parlor. His face was still the same ghastly pallor, but his voice was strong and assured.

"It's time for you to be upstairs with Jane," I said quietly. I could see the comment register and was sure John knew what I meant, but he didn't reply to it, instead handed me the penciled scrawl. He had done a masterful job. Every movement he and his wife had made during the past week was carefully chronicled, right down to the hour of their bedtime and rising. Under any other conditions I would have been hesitant to peer into another's privacy so completely, but these conditions were anything but normal.

"As you can see," he said, pointing over my shoulder at the list, "I started on Friday last and worked my way through."

"Thank you, John. This may be what we need."

"Can you read my writing?"

"Oh yes. Indeed. Let me go over this. If I have any questions, I'll come up and ask."

Bannerman nodded and then seemed to slump. He glanced at the stairway, out in the hall, and then at me.

"Nothing can be done?"

"I'm afraid not." I sighed. "There are some diseases that we've made progress with over the years, but I'm sorry to say that anthrax isn't one of them. She is resting comfortably, though, I think, and feels no pain. She was unconscious when I came down."

Bannerman laid a hand on my arm. "Thank you, Robert."

"There's nothing to thank me for."

I watched Bannerman's broad back, hunched with misery, as he went up the stairs to be with his wife. I knew there was no hope, and somehow that thought brought to mind that I had not attended the funeral that afternoon for the little Servin girl. It was a thought I tried not to dwell on for long.

John Bannerman's list was nearly three pages, and I sat down, lighted a cigar, and began at the top, ticking off each item with a pencil John had left.

The incubation period for anthrax was wildly variable but, compared with some other virulent diseases, was incredibly rapid—from scarcely a day to perhaps as long as four or five days. Both Jane Bannerman and the man from the cooperage had what I believed to be an infection beginning in the intestinal track. Neither one had showed signs of the vicious lung congestion and destruction that had felled the two cowboys at the camp. That might come later, I thought soberly. Jane Bannerman was showing that evening a general collapse of her entire system, and I knew she was near the end.

With that in mind, I scanned John Bannerman's list, looking for a likely time when their food may have been contaminated or when they might have come in contact with contaminated animals. I concentrated on the food aspect, because that was where I believed the woman's infection had begun. There was an immediate problem. John Bannerman, thankfully, had not contracted the disease. Nothing in my studies had led me to believe that the anthrax was the least bit capricious, however. If John Bannerman had eaten food infected with the spores, he would have been felled by the disease. It was as simple as that.

The Bannerman diary read like it was—a reflection of the life of a genteel couple who minded their own business. They did not entertain very much and in fact had had no guests to dinner during the week he had chronicled.

One item did catch my attention quickly, however. On the previous Monday evening, perhaps for a change of pace, the couple had gone out to dinner. They had eaten at the Branding Iron, a place as close to fashionable as the village was able to boast. On Tuesday the Servin girl had been killed, and it was Wednesday morning when Bannerman had cornered me in the street, pleading with me to look at his ill wife. Nowhere else in the list, as detailed as it was, lay any other clue. They had not gone riding, either mounted or in a carriage. They had not visited any other household in the village. They owned no livestock of their own, not even a dog or cat. In comparison with all the other entries—notations of work, doing laundry, baking, cleaning house, sitting quietly in the evening and reading, one short stroll through the cottonwood grove behind their home in the quiet of a Saturday evening—the one entry that involved the Branding Iron stood out as an event singular and unexpected.

I circled the entry and put out my cigar, walking quickly to the stairway.

Bannerman was sitting beside the bed, holding his wife's hand. She was still unconscious, and the banker did not take his eyes from her face when I entered the room.

"John," I said softly, and he turned. After a moment, he stood with effort, placing his wife's hand on the coverlet. He walked over to me and raised an eyebrow in his characteristic questioning expression.

"I ask you to excuse this intrusion," I said, but he waved a hand in impatient dismissal, nodding at the paper I held instead. "I need to know about your dinner at the Branding Iron on Monday evening."

He looked at the list, focusing on the circled entry, the entry that said they had enjoyed themselves during a brief night on the town.

"Our anniversary," Bannerman said, his voice emotionless.

"Christ," I said and looked away for a minute. Then, "What did you eat?"

He put both hands to his forehead, as if he could press the thoughts out of his skull. "I had trout," he said, speaking through his hands. "I haven't been able to take the time to go fishing for so long." He took down his hands and looked at me. "It was so good."

"And Jane?"

"She loves a good steak," he said hollowly. "She had one so big she couldn't finish it, and for her, that's something."

I looked down, folding the list carefully, and started to put it in my pocket. I was not thinking about Jane Bannerman just then, or the other two cowboys, or the laborer. I was remembering that I had ordered a steak at the Branding Iron the night Becky Servin had been killed. I had not been able to eat it. A chill ran up my spine as I realized that if the meat had been infected with anthrax spores, and I had been hungry, I would be at death's door myself.

"Maybe that's it, then," I said, looking down at the list. I glanced at Bannerman. "Maybe the meat was tainted."

"She didn't say it tasted bad," Bannerman said quietly. He shook his head again. "I don't believe any of this is happening," he said hopelessly.

"We've got to know," I said and tapped the list. There was nothing I could do for Jane Bannerman then, but I moved toward the bed. The banker caught me by the arm and turned me around.

"Robert," he said, "why don't you go? You need to track this thing down before anybody else . . ." and his voice trailed off. I started to say something, but he shook his head. "I need . . . I need to be alone with her." He looked at me, and his eyes were tortured. "Others need you more. There's nothing you can do, is there?"

I clicked my black bag shut, picking it up from where it had been sitting near the foot of the bed. "I'll return as soon as I can," I said and thrust out my hand. Bannerman's grasp was dry and powerful, and then I left, feeling like a scoundrel.

CHAPTER 5

To do what needed doing, there should have been three of me, but such was not the case. It was after ten o'clock, and most of the evening bustle of the village had quieted down—just a distant nicker of a lonesome horse or the yip of a dog. I wanted to find the man who had come to my office earlier. He might add to my information already gleaned from John Bannerman. If the restaurant was to blame, a second case of poisoning from food would confirm it.

The narrow lane that passed by the Bannermans' cut from the main street of Cooperville across a small hillock to the cooperage itself.

That industry was the pride of the village. Jonas Caldwell owned it and supplied barrels, tanks, buckets—virtually anything that would hold liquids—as well as the finest wagon and buggy wheels in the Rocky Mountains. That was Caldwell's claim, anyway, and his prosperity seemed to bear him out. He employed more than two dozen workers, had built the business up from nothing more than a tent-town blacksmith's shop. It was one of those two dozen workers I was concerned about.

It was pitch dark walking along the lane, and the trees prevented any moon from making the going any easier. I cracked my elbow against more than one tree trunk but eventually found myself standing in front of the towering, dark hulk of the cooperage.

I knew no one would be working at that hour but hoped Caldwell would be home. He lived in a house nearly taller than it was wide, a narrow, dark, angular house that seemed tacked to the rear of the cooperage. I made my way around the front of the mill, praying there were no guard dogs that would mind my presence, and turned the corner. His house was dark, a shadowy hulk up the hill, but one light shone yellow out a back window of the second story of the mill, and I made for that.

Because the cooperage mill sat on the hill, the front was two stories. But the back, where I then stood, was only one, the ground rising up to just under the yellow window. I peered through the dusty, filthy glass and saw Jonas Caldwell, back toward me, working at a desk littered with more paper than I thought possible. Any tremor would have sent the papers off the desk in a landslide. I gently rapped on the window, and Caldwell turned, peering over his glasses with brow furrowed.

"It's Dr. Patterson," I shouted. "I need to talk with you."

"Well then, come on in," Caldwell said, just loud enough for me to hear.

"Where's the door?"

For the first time the man smiled. His teeth were rotten. "Just keep a goin' round back."

I nodded and found the door, pulling it open against the protest of unoiled iron hinges. It opened into a short hallway, and I could see the light from Caldwell's office streaming out. He had turned around but still stared at me as I entered, glasses low on his nose.

"I was workin' late," he announced, as if not the least surprised at a visit from the village doctor at that hour.

"I need to know where one of your men is, Mr. Caldwell."

"That so?" He leaned back in the chair, tipping it so that the back rested against the wall by the window. He was burly, thick-armed and thick-necked, with a flushed face that looked like he had a perpetual fever.

"Yes. Maybe you can help me. The man I need is tall, strong-built, light hair, freckles. He's sick, and I didn't get his name when he came to my office."

"Kinda late to be makin' rounds, ain't it?"

"He needs help."

Caldwell thumped forward, the legs hitting the floor hard. The mass of papers shifted, but he ignored them.

"I got nearly thirty men work for me. Lots of 'em big, lots of 'em strong." He grinned rottenly.

"This man couldn't have come to work the past day or so." I thought wildly about more details that might ring a bell with this man. "Real light-colored hair. Lots of freckles. Ah . . ." I stopped. I hadn't paid enough attention to the patient the first time around to see any better picture of him.

"Hmm," Caldwell hummed. "Might be Sandy Bascomb. He's a towhead. That's why they call him Sandy, as you might well imagine." He hesitated. "Or Gus Wharton. But Gus was in the mill today. I talked to him. If he was sick, he did a good job of hidin' the fact. Course, some men are like that. Don't want to miss work. Love that dollar."

"Where's this Bascomb fellow live, then?" I pressed. If Wharton was working, he wasn't the one I was after.

"This fella have a mustache?"

"No."

"Then it's not Wharton. He's got a mustache. Must be Bascomb."

"You know where he lives, then?" I repeated.

"Sure. I think he's in one of those shacks that string along the crick up into the timber. He told me once he had him a woman and was gonna move down near here somewheres, where us rich folk live." He grinned again. "But he never did."

As quickly as possible, I thanked Caldwell and left. The shacks he had referred to were half a dozen in number, walking up the steep hillside across the valley from the cooperage, a quarter of a mile away. The shacks had been built years before by a man who had grand ideas about mining the small ribbon of a creek that came down out of the hills.

Stumbling in the dark, I was out of breath by the time I reached the creek, and I followed it up the hillside, avoiding the small junipers and larger pines and stumps that loomed out of the dark. A light glowed softly from one shack; the rest were smudges against the inky hillside. I made for the light.

I pounded on the door urgently and was rewarded by a shout of annoyance.

"Open that damn door before you break it!"

An old gnarled man sat at a rough, handmade table, a bottle of wine in front of him. He was playing solitaire, a blackened corncob pipe dangling from his lips. I was surprised that I didn't recognize him, by face if not by name.

"Chester Rogers," he said by way of introduction. He did not stand up. "Howdy and set."

"I'm Dr. Patterson, from down in the village," I said, not "setting."

"Know who you are. Seen you from time to time. Ain't never been sick, so you don't know me. One of these days, though." He clicked his tongue and put the two of spades on the ace. I would have liked to have spent time with Rogers, finding out how he supported himself and his cards, but I couldn't spare the time.

"I need to find Sandy Bascomb," I said. "You know which ah . . . house is his?"

"Sandy?"

"Yes. Sandy Bascomb. Works down at the cooperage."

"I know it."

"You know where he lives?"

"Sure enough do. What's your business with him?"

I flushed with anger, wondering why everyone that night wanted to play questions with me. Rogers turned another card with deliberate care and found the three of spades.

"That's none of your business, Mr. Rogers," I snapped. "I need him and fast. I can take time and check every shack on the hill, or you can help me out by telling me straightaway."

Rogers looked up through his thick eyebrows. "Now ain't we hoity-toity, though," he said matter-of-factly. He slapped down the cards and stood up with great care, old joints protesting. His back stayed bent. He went to what passed for a window and pointed out into the darkness. "There's a shack right over there, a hundred yards or so. That ain't his. The one behind it is."

"Thank you," I said abruptly and walked out.

"You come back when you ain't in such an all-fired hurry, young fella," Rogers called after me.

I trotted as fast as I dared through the darkness, the juniper limbs tearing at my clothes from time to time. I

passed the house that wasn't Bascomb's and reached the
one that was. It was dark. But I knew what was inside.
Those shacks weren't built particularly snug. Air could
flow in through a hundred cracks. In this case the air
flowed out, poisonous and pungent. I groped in my pockets for my matches, found three, and struck them all at
once on my trouser leg, pushing open the unlocked door
as I did so. The smell of the place came charging out and
I recoiled. The matches flickered and threatened to go
out, and I cupped them with my hand, steeling myself to
enter the shack. I could see Bascomb on a cot along the
near wall. He was dead and had been for more than a
day. The combination of the anthrax and a day of warm
temperatures had done nothing pretty to the man. I
covered my nose and mouth with one hand and retreated, snapping out the matches. I remembered to
close the door before I made my way back down the hill.
On the way I wondered what Bascomb's last thoughts
had been . . . whether he had cursed doctors and medicine for killing him so effectively.

But had he eaten at the Branding Iron restaurant? I
resolved to visit the restaurant and made my way toward
the heart of the sleeping village. I wasn't tired yet and
was even somewhat irked that most of the citizenry of
Cooperville had gone to bed. If I had to pound on doors
and wake up half the village for answers, I was prepared
to do so.

The Branding Iron was an unpretentious place, no
more than two smallish rooms of tables and a separate
kitchen. There was a boarding house besides, but with a
separate entrance. The restaurant was closed, but the
lights were on. I tried the door, rattling the latch, and

saw Marion Smith coming across through the tables. She opened the door something less than cheerfully.

"Dinner was some hours ago," she observed dryly but held the door open for me to enter. She looked at me critically, no doubt smelling the sweat. "But you're not here to eat."

"No. Is Tom here?"

"He's baking in the back."

I started to cross the room, and Marion said, "I hear word that Mrs. Bannerman is gravely ill."

"I need to talk with Tom," I said again. Mrs. Smith was a professional gossip, and I had no desire to feed her need just then. She frowned and wiped her hands on her apron. I turned and made for the kitchen.

Thomas Smith, so thin that he was almost transparent, was laboring in the sweltering heat of the wood range, and the sweet smell of baked goods was enough to make my mouth water even then. On top of the stove sat another masterpiece, a large pot of beef stew, bubbling and gurgling. The gaunt cook, one of the few such in the world, I was sure, stirred the stew, squinted at the thermometer in the door of the oven, and then turned to me, his face attentive.

"Would you excuse us?" I said, looking at Marion and knowing I was offending her. I felt it necessary. She stalked out of the kitchen without a word.

"Whatsa problem, Doc?" Smith said then, and he leaned against a heavy butcher-block table, hands pale from washing dishes, sleeves rolled up almost to his elbows. Out of habit, I looked at his arms and then almost cursed aloud.

"Let me see that arm, Tom." I reached over, taking

him by the wrist. He fought my grip for a moment out of confusion, then let me look.

"What the hell's so important about a boil or two?" he said. "You makin' rounds for boils this time of night?" I examined the three papules, their centers dark and the surrounding inflammation livid.

"Tom, somehow there's bad beef in town, and I think you've got it here."

"Now see here," he said, drawing himself up righteously. "Just what do you mean by that?"

"Three people have died of anthrax, and another will before the day is over. That," and I pointed at his arm, "is anthrax."

"Son of a bitch, this is a sorry joke," Smith nearly bellowed. "If you wasn't so high thought of, I'd throw you right out of this here kitchen."

I outweighed Smith by fifty pounds and towered over him by five inches, so I let him blow off steam. When his string of curses subsided, I said, "Tom, I'm sure as I can be. Sandy Bascomb ever eat here?"

Smith looked like he was about to snap out a negative answer, then apparently thought better of it. "Course he does. All the time."

"In the past four or five days?"

"Well . . . sure. He eats here most every night. Haven't seen him in the past few days, but he's a regular. What's that got to do with it?"

"Sandy Bascomb is dead, Tom. Anthrax killed him."

Tom Smith's face went blank, and he leaned against the table a little harder. "He's dead?"

I nodded. "Sometime late yesterday or early today."

"Well . . . well . . . that don't mean he got it here, by God." Smith shook his head. "Damn. He was a good

man, Doc. But that don't mean he got it here!" There
was almost a note of panic in the cook's voice then.

"Tom, look at your arm. For God's sake, man, those
aren't simple boils. Now time's wasting. You need help,
and we've got to make sure this thing doesn't spread."

Smith held up a hand. "Now, hold on, young fella. Just
how are you so all fired sure it's here the trouble starts?"

"You remember the Bannermans eating here? Monday night? It was their anniversary. Mrs. Bannerman had
steak, her husband had fish. Jane Bannerman is dying of
anthrax, John isn't. Bascomb died of it. He ate here. You
own the place and," I pointed at the arm again, "you've
got it. Where did you get the beef? Let me tell you. I
think you purchased it, maybe a head or two, from three
men, one of them named Jensen, one named Brown.
Two of those men are dead too, Tom. And one of their
horses."

Thomas Smith looked at the bubbling pot on the stove.
"That there's some of the meat too," he said, subdued.

"Then get rid of it. Bury it. How many have eaten
meat from the steer you bought?"

Smith looked at me, dejected, knowing the truth.
"They had six head, you know. I don't know if they told
you that, Doc. Or how you found out. But I paid for one,
figured I'd put it in the ice house for winter. Cut off a few
steaks, some for this stew."

"Where did the other five go?"

Smith shrugged. "I told Jensen that Corey Staples, east
of here, was looking to buy some stock for his spread.
Young fella, you know, lookin' for stock at a good price to
build his herd, what there is of it."

"The other five went out there?"

"I guess. Course, I ain't got no way of knowing for sure. But damn it, Doc, you sure about all this?"

"It's the only way it can be, Tom. You've got to close down."

"Close down? What in hell for?"

"Because you got the damn anthrax right here in your restaurant! How much more reason do you need? How many people out there have had the beef?"

Smith started to rub his arm, then thought better of it. "None, Doc. Cept what you say. I been paying a bunch of youngsters a dime each for every trout they bring in that tops sixteen inches. Folks really go for that. And I shot me an elk last week. They're a big animal. Folks say it's better than beef anyways. Now me, I never cared for beef. This bein' cattle country, I guess a man could get hung for sayin' that, but I never had a real hankerin' for it."

"Then that saved your life, Tom. You butcher the beef yourself?"

"Why sure. Ain't nothing to that."

"And you haven't had any of that stew?"

"No, it ain't near ready yet."

"Thank God for that. You got an external infection."

"What?"

"Those," I said pointing.

"They ain't nothing," he said, still willing to believe that maybe his luck would change.

"They'll kill you as sure as we're standing here if something's not done."

"I ain't going to close this restaurant, Doc. All I got's in this place. A thing like this gets out, and I won't have a customer. Ever."

"Tom," I said, "I hate to do this, but by God, I'll have this place closed by the law if you don't do it willingly."

Smith glared at me, standing straight, hands balled in fists. "Now don't you go telling me what to do! Not you, not anybody!"

I held up both hands. "Tom, understand this. We don't have time. If you don't cooperate, you will be dead in five days' time. Do you understand me? That infection on your arm, if it hasn't already, will spread into your system. This isn't the grippe or a little bowel trouble we're talking about. It's anthrax, Tom, and there is no cure once it's inside your gut. No cure at all. None. How you managed to avoid getting the dust in your lungs, I don't know. You're a lucky man, Tom. But don't push it. Every minute you spend in here, you are endangering those innocent folks out there." I waved a hand at the door to the dining room. "Think on that, Tom. There's four dead already. You want to be number five? You want one of those customers of yours to be number six?"

Tom Smith glared at me and then dropped his gaze to the floor. He shook his head wearily. "Shit," he said, just barely audible. "How was I to know? Cow's a cow. And now they's out at Staples'." He turned, reached down, and flipped the damper closed on the kitchen range.

"Tell me what I gotta do," he said.

"We need to get rid of the beef," I replied, "and the stew. I don't know about the elk, but let's be safe. Get rid of that too."

"They been eatin' that right along."

"But it's stored in the ice house, with the beef?"

"Course it is."

"Then let's get rid of it."

A little of Smith's fire came back momentarily. "Doc, if you're wrong in this . . ."

"I'm not wrong, Tom. And another thing, you be in my office in ten minutes."

"Now what the hell for?"

I pointed at his arm. "That's what for. You take ten minutes to explain things to Marion. Make sure she understands. Has she handled any of the beef?"

"No," he said sullenly. "She don't cook."

"No, but she's been around you. She have any boils?"

"No."

"If she does, I want to see her too. For the time being I'll settle for you, if she has been feeling fine. You don't have to tell her it's anthrax if you don't want to."

"Ain't no point in hidin' it now, is there?"

"No, I guess not. But I'm serious about getting rid of the meat. All of it. You sure no one else has had any of the beef? Yesterday? The day before?"

Smith shook his head. "Like I said, the fish and elk. Been good sellers."

"Ten minutes then, in my office. Bring a nightshirt, because you'll be there until at least tomorrow."

"Doc," Smith protested, "you know what goddamned time it is? It's the middle of the night. Can't you wait 'till tomorrow?"

"No. You can't wait, Tom." I turned to go. "Ten minutes, Tom. That's all. If you're not there, I'll come with help to get you."

Smith laughed helplessly. "Ain't no call to make threats. I'll be there."

CHAPTER 6

When I trudged up to the door of my office, I saw a note tucked into a crack of the jamb. I pulled it out and immediately recognized John Bannerman's scrawl in the light of a struck match. I shook out the match, fumbled my skeleton key into the lock, and let myself in.

I lighted several lamps, then looked at the message, signed most formally with the full, flowing signature of the banker.

Robert:
Jane died no more than an hour after you left. Forgive me for not calling for you at that time. But as you said, there was nothing for you here. You have my support and assistance and resources for anything you may need. Kindly stop by this evening, no matter the hour, should you find a moment.

I read the message again and said a mental farewell to a woman I had liked and respected and wondered at the same time what kind of iron the will of her husband was forged from. That he should mention asking forgiveness from me at such a time told me in no uncertain terms that I did not know John Bannerman as well as I had thought.

I carefully folded the note, thrust it in my pocket, and made preparations. Hoping that Thomas Smith would be prompt, I went to my examining room and took down the Whittaker volume. If the anthrax hadn't dug its way into Smith's vitals, but still lurked only in the skin, then there was a faint chance his life might be saved. At least, I found myself thinking, let him live long enough to provide some more answers.

Jensen, Brown, and the third, unknown cowpuncher had herded the six infected cattle from somewhere, perhaps leaving another herd that was also infected. One of the cattle was accounted for. Five more, Smith had said, were probably headed for the range of another innocent rancher.

What haunted me just then was the incredible cold-bloodedness of the man Brown. Taking cattle he knew to be sick, then selling one to a restaurant, taking the easy money, and then herding the remaining steers to another ranch. If my notions of the timing of the incident were correct, the two cowboys had become sick after disposing of the cattle. After waiting fatally long, Brown had come to town for a doctor, a last-ditch effort to do something for his stricken friends. But then he had ridden off, taking not only his own mount but another man's as well. And why had he used his partner's name when introducing himself to me? I fervently hoped that Thomas Smith might have some of the answers, for Brown was long gone, leaving behind him a wake of ravaged corpses.

I was pressed for time, but I resolved to make sure that I set the law after Brown. The only law was Vince McCuskar, and that thought didn't make me feel any better. I thought about the Staples ranch, where Smith had said the other five head of sick cattle were headed. But it was dark, and in all likelihood the cattle would be mixed in with the rest of the herd—impossible to sort out in the dead of night. That problem would have to wait for first light.

I had everything prepared by the time Thomas Smith knocked tentatively at my door. I ushered him in. He was nervous and kept glancing around the examining room apprehensively as if it was a kind of butcher shop and he was the beef.

"Sit down, Tom," I said gently. He did so, hands clasped like a child. "Take off your shirt, if you would." Smith started to unbutton his shirt, then glanced out the window and hesitated. I reached over and lowered the blind so our privacy was assured.

I looked at him critically. "Tom," I said, standing directly in front of him, "do you know anything at all about anthrax?"

"No," he said slowly, "sure don't. But I can tell you one thing, Doc . . . I got me an account to settle with that fella."

"You may have to stand in line," I said.

"There ain't no cure, is there?"

I tried to sound encouraging. "It's not as bad as all that," I lied, then qualified that fib with something close to a half-truth. "If the infection is just in the skin, like yours, then there is a great deal we can do. That's why I was so harsh with you earlier, demanding that you come to see me for treatment."

Smith nodded. "That's all right, Doc. You got your job to do."

"The trouble is, the skin, or external infection, doesn't simply go away. At least in most cases it doesn't. The treatment is something that is necessary, believe me. There will be considerable pain afterward, but you'll be up and about in no time, I'm sure. You're a strong man."

"How much is it gonna cost?"

I laughed aloud at the incongruity of that. "Not a cent, Thomas, as long as you get well. Now, off with that shirt."
He finished disrobing, and I counted seven skin eruptions, the three on his left arm I had seen earlier, another at the top of his shoulder joint, and three more in the deep muscle at the base of his neck. Some of my confidence sagged at the sight of the papules, for the ones on his upper body lay dangerously close to major vessels, where the infection had ready access to the rest of his system.

"You had any chills, fever, coughing spells?"

He shook his head.

"Any dizziness? Any pain in the gut or the lungs?"

"Nope. Them boils hurt some, but that's about all."

"I would think they would. Now," I smoothed the rubber cover on the small operating table, "I want you up here, on your belly, head at that end." As short as Smith was, the table was still shorter. I called it an operating table, but it was nothing so fancy. Underneath, it was simple slab wood, with stout, turned legs I had had made by the cooperage. Smith looked at the table skeptically.

"Can't I just set here?"

"No," I said, taking him by the elbow. "It's a little hard for me to work. And I wouldn't want you falling out of the chair on your face."

"I ain't gonna faint."

"No, you certainly aren't, but you're going to be sound asleep, and it's difficult sleeping when you're sitting bolt upright."

He looked at me, uneasy again. "Sleep?"

"Yes, I'll use the ether."

"Oh no you don't. I heard about that, and you ain't gonna do that to me."

"Tom, listen." I leaned against the table, wondering again how there could be such advances in the practice of medicine but so little in the attitude of patients. "Those aren't ordinary boils that we can just lance and let it go at that. The infection has to come out, all of it. I will have to cut pretty deep, removing the entire papule and some of the surrounding tissue."

"You got a bottle of whiskey?"

I sighed. "This isn't some Civil War battlefield, Tom. We don't put a leather belt between your teeth and hope your nerves are made of steel. Believe me, you'll be fine in no time, and you won't even know what happened."

He still looked dubious and hadn't made a move to leave his chair. I couldn't spare any more time.

"Thomas, do you trust me? You want help? No, let me put it this way. Do you want to live?"

"Well sure."

"Then get up on that goddamned table and stop arguing with me!" I snapped. He looked at me in surprise. "You want me to pick you up and put you there?" At that, he gave me a sheepish, appraising look, knowing full well I could do as I threatened.

He rose from the chair and went to the table, swung a leg up, and then lay down on his belly, as I had asked.

"Thank you," I muttered. In another minute or so Thomas Smith was out cold, put in happy slumber by the ether that I held to his face on a piece of saturated linen.

I worked on his arm first, excising the diseased masses carefully. I cut down to the healthy tissue deep below the papules, rinsing the scalpel frequently in the concentrated carbolic acid that sloshed in a shallow metal enamel pan at my side. After each lesion was removed, I applied a powder of corrosive sublimate, a substance that acted as a chemical cautery. As I did so, I again blessed the action of the ether. The pain would be severe enough when Smith awoke. The final treatment was something Dr. Whittaker had mentioned in his writings, a treatment that had been tried to some effect in Italy. Using the hypodermic, I injected a three-percent solution of carbolic acid into the tissue underneath the site of each anthrax manifestation. Each area was then bandaged in sterile linen, the cloth soaked in a combination of carbolic acid and iodine.

It was a messy, radical, and time-consuming treatment. I spent more time than I liked on the lesions on his neck, particularly one that lay altogether too close to the spine. In that case, I modified the destructive action of the sublimate by an admixture of that powder with a proportion of calomel. When I completed the treatment at last, I looked at my watch. I had been working on Smith for nearly an hour and a half. The smell of ether mixed with the other chemicals in the small room, and I went to the window, opening it for some fresh air. Turning back to look at my patient, I was disturbed by the sight of him. He looked like a soldier who had stood in front of a Gatling gun with a fair marksman at the trigger. I took his pulse and heard it, strong and regular.

I took a moment to examine the rest of his body but found no more infections. A matter of two or three days would tell the story. I had beaten the external infection, I knew that. If the disease had spread within, there was nothing more I could do. I put a woolen blanket over Smith to keep the chill off him. It would be several minutes before he came out of the last application of ether and then he would be in considerable pain. I needed to be there and so resigned myself to the wait. I went to the front door, opened it, and stood on the step smoking a cigar. The town was dead-quiet. I glanced at my watch again and saw it was nearly one in the morning. I sighed, snapped the watch closed, and looked down the street, toward the lane that led to the Bannerman home. The neighbors would have been visiting in droves, and, I knew, John Bannerman would have politely received them all, taking their condolences, putting the dishes of food for which he had no appetite in neat rows in the kitchen. Some of it would spoil, some would be picked at . . . and then I sucked in my breath sharply, astonished at my own stupidity.

I was about to leave Thomas Smith when I saw Marion's stout figure, a dark blot against the street, coming toward me. I walked briskly toward her, and even in the darkness I could see the worry on her face.

"Tom's fine, Marion," I said. "He's not out of the ether, and I need to ask you a favor."

She halted and squinted up at me. "At this hour?"

"It can't wait."

"Then?"

"I need to be here when Thomas wakes up from the ether, but it's imperative that I talk with Ruben Blumenthal."

"Now?"

"Yes, ma'am. Now. Could I ask you . . ."

"I'll fetch him. I dare say he won't take kindly to being aroused in the dead of night, but I'll fetch him." Without another word she turned and made for Blumenthal's, no more than a hundred yards away. She hadn't asked why I needed to see the mortician, and I was grateful for that. I breathed a sigh of relief and went back inside. Tom was beginning to stir, and I made sure I had a sterile hypodermic and the opiates at hand.

I don't know what Marion Smith told the undertaker, but he was thumping into my office, Mrs. Smith in tow, within ten minutes. He hadn't taken any great pains with his dress, and his thinning hair was rumpled from sleep. He stopped, squinting against even the mellow light from the lanterns, and looked at Smith.

"That Tom?" he asked.

"Yes. He'll be fine." Blumenthal nodded curtly.

"Marion, perhaps you'd like to sit with Tom." I motioned toward a chair, then took the undertaker by the arm and steered him back outside where we had some privacy. I closed the door of my office behind me.

"Thanks for coming, Ruben," I began. Blumenthal was still breathing heavily from his exertion, and I reflected that if he was to shed some of his two hundred fifty pounds, his five-foot, seven-inch frame would be considerably more comfortable.

"You keep some long hours, Doctor," he said. "Mrs. Smith was somewhat, ah, adamant that I get my old carcass out of bed."

"It's about the Bannerman woman," I said, and he nodded.

"Couple of John's neighbors brought the body over shortly after she died."

"I know. Did . . ."

Blumenthal interrupted me, holding up a hand. "There come a note with the body, Doctor. It's all taken care of."

"A note?"

"Mr. Bannerman sent a note saying what she died of.

That's all I needed to know. I got me some boys out of bed, and they dug deep. We limed the grave after that."

"Thank God," I said. "I'm glad someone is thinking straight."

Blumenthal smiled slightly, his pudgy face unlined and ruddy. "There's a few of us that's been around for a while," he said. "No offense intended."

I told Blumenthal about Sandy Bascomb, up in the shack, and he frowned.

"Seems like the best thing to do is just set the shack afire," he said and scratched his head. "Maybe get the parson to say a couple words first. Bascomb didn't have no relatives hereabouts, least not as far as I know." He looked up at me, a sideways glance, waiting to see what I would say.

"That would seem the best thing," I said nodding. "If you can do that without setting the mountain on fire. That would prevent the contagion from spreading anywhere beyond the shack."

"I'll get some of the boys tomorrow, first light. And that ain't long from now," he said and grinned. "We'll take care of it, Doctor. Don't worry none."

"I appreciate that."

"Tom got the anthrax?"

"Smith?"

"Uh-huh."

"He's got an external infection. I think he'll live. There were two cowboys that died of it, but that was some distance from here. I think they're the ones that brought it into town."

"Hell of a thing," Blumenthal said. "Hell of a thing. Well," and he hitched his trousers up over his massive gut, "if I'm to be up first light, then I got me some serious

sleepin' to do. Just now got to bed." He stopped.
"There's quite a bit of gossip going around this town,
Doctor, but all in all, I think folks is taking it pretty well.
Some are kind of nervous, but then they always are
around me. So who's to tell?"

He chuckled dryly and touched his forehead. "Have a
good night, Doctor. Give my best to Mrs. Smith."

I watched the fat figure of the undertaker plod off into
the darkness and then turned to go back inside.

Marion Smith sat, ramrod straight, beside the table
where her husband lay, still out cold.

"Thomas will be fine now?" she said, her voice emotionless.

"I think so."

"You think?" She looked at me coldly, assessing. She
still hadn't forgiven me for snubbing her at the restaurant earlier.

"You know what his illness is, I presume," I said. "You
know it's dangerous."

"Of course I know," she snapped and got up. "Whole
town knows."

"Perhaps that's best. Ignorance is no defense against
something like this. It had to be done."

She let that pass. Her husband stirred and groaned and
then tried, more out of reflex than anything else, to roll
over. I put a hand on his good shoulder and restrained
him.

"He'll have to lie still for a while, until he's fully
regained his senses. We don't want him hurting himself.
There will be enough pain without that."

"I'll get him home and take care of him," Marion said.
She was standing close to her husband.

"It would be better if he stayed here. He needs careful watching for the next day or two."

"I'm not capable of that?"

I could argue with her husband, but Marion was beyond me. I shrugged and gave up. "It will be another hour or two before he's strong enough to walk home," I said. "Let me give you some medicine if he's in too much pain."

"Brandy will work as well as anything else," Marion said crisply, and she laid a hand on her husband's forehead. Her sudden show of warmth toward the man surprised me.

"Ma'am, let me impress upon you the importance of keeping a vigilant eye on his condition for the next forty-eight hours or so. Any fever, any sign of . . . well, anything other than some expected pain, you come and fetch me."

"I'll remember that, Doctor," she said. "I shan't have much else to do. No one will be hungry, at least not enough to eat at the Branding Iron."

"I'm sorry."

Marion shook her head. "Some vacation won't hurt, and folks have short memories."

"Something still must be done about the beef in your ice house," I said.

"It's been done, Doctor. I had two men carry the carcass out and burn it with coal oil. The stew as well." She clucked. "Such a dreadful waste. But it's done. Oh, and the elk meat too, just as Thomas said. All burned."

"The men touched the carcass?"

She looked at me as if I was strange. "How else can it be carried? They wore gloves and then burned those as well. You needn't worry. And I, after the last of them left the restaurant, spent the night cleaning the kitchen. Every surface," she said proudly, "every surface I scrubbed with lime in water." She held up two hands that looked like poached eggs. "There will be no more problem," she said.

"You would like something for your hands? They must be tender."

"I used gloves and burned them also. My hands will mend, I assure you."

The relief I felt knew no measure, and I looked at this tough, brusque woman in a new light.

"Mrs. Smith, I owe you thanks and an apology. A heartfelt apology."

For the first time, she came close to smiling. "Nonsense. When you've been around as long as I have, you'll learn to take things in stride. Now, I'll just make myself comfortable here with Thomas, and then when he's fit we'll go home. You have other things to do, I'm sure. You'd best be about them." And with that she plumped herself down again, near the head of the table on which the half-conscious Thomas lay, dismissing me from my own office as if she owned the world.

"If anyone should call for me, tell them I'll be with Marshal McCuskar for a bit. Then I'll be over with John Bannerman."

"No one will call at this hour of the night," Marion said crisply, eyes still on her husband.

"Well, if they do," I said. Marion Smith nodded without looking my way, and I left the office, closing the door quietly behind me. I wanted to be with Bannerman, but time was slipping by. If McCuskar could be of any help, each second would count. The grieving banker would have to wait a little longer.

CHAPTER 7

There were few people, myself included, who looked favorably on being jolted out of a sound sleep. But I took almost a perverse pleasure in rousting Vincent McCuskar out of bed. From the glazed look in his eyes, I could see he had been in a deep slumber, unmindful of what had been going on in his own town.

He came to the loose-fitting door of his room, a small, dark, and cramped affair in the rear of the marshal's office and jail. He was in his long johns, buttons straining to cover his tubby belly. He scratched in a couple places, looking me up and down as he held the door open.

"I have to talk to you," I said, not apologizing for the hour.

"It could wait for mornin'," he grumbled and didn't offer to let me into his room.

"It can't wait, McCuskar," I snapped. "Let me spell it out for you. A man, I think his name is Brown, sold diseased cattle, one head to Tom Smith, the others maybe to Corey Staples. There's been four died from it. I have every reason to believe the man Brown knew full well what he was doing. That makes him subject to the law."

McCuskar almost sneered. He didn't like me much, especially in the middle of the night. "Subject to the law, hell," he said, voice hoarse.

"Yes, Marshal, subject to the law. I want him caught

and brought to justice. You're marshal here. That's your job." I glanced around, then leaned closer. "And I don't give a good goddamn about the hour."

McCuskar straightened up, trying to suck his belly in. It was hard for him to be dignified any time, but in his present condition, even more so.

"Patterson, you got a long nose for other folks' business," he rasped. "But suppose I give you another five seconds before I slam this here door in your face. You tell me just what law this Brown fella has broke, and I'll tell ya what I aim to do about it."

"Four dead doesn't mean anything?"

"What's the law, wise man?" He rubbed his nose and then spat on the ground. "Man sells a sick cow, then it's the buyer's lookout, seems to me."

I cursed under my breath. "Brown knew the cattle were sick, Marshal."

"Did Smith ask him if they was sick? No. You buy a horse from a man, he don't have to tell you a thing, 'less you ask. Smith didn't ask." His eyes bored into mine. "So maybe you'll just trot on and leave me be."

"And that's it?"

"That's it, sonny boy."

I almost punched him. I stood silently for a moment, exchanging glares, trying to figure out what to say that might do some good. I remembered the calmness of Brown, when he had come to fetch me, and when he had gathered his gear and ridden out of his camp, leaving his two partners dying. Brown and McCuskar wouldn't have been much of a fair match. But right then, I almost wished Brown would walk around the corner, ready for a showdown. I would have helped serve McCuskar up to him on a platter.

"A man kills four people that easy, he'll kill again, Marshal," I said, trying to keep my voice level.

McCuskar, feeling himself on higher ground, just shrugged. "He comes into town and steps out of line, then I'll deal with him," he said nonchalantly.

"He's not apt to come back," I said. "Seems like it would be your job to tail after him."

McCuskar laughed, not kindly. "You sure are an ignorant cuss," he said. "What's outside of this town ain't my jurisdiction. He ain't broke no law in town. Simple as that."

"You're a little short on nerve," I said softly, and McCuskar squinted, catching my meaning full well. But he didn't say anything. I turned on my heel and stalked off, fists clenched. Maybe John Bannerman would have some answers. Maybe the county sheriff would do what Vince McCuskar was unwilling to do—track down Brown and make sure he didn't kill anyone else. As I walked quickly toward John Bannerman's home, deep in the darkness of the cottonwoods, I knew that two dangerous plagues were loose—one of them was anthrax, something I understood. But the other was a cold-blooded killer named Brown, and there was nothing in any of my medical books that offered a solution for him.

"Look at all this, Robert. Can you imagine?" John Bannerman gestured halfheartedly at the array of foodstuffs that was lined up in the Bannerman kitchen, everything from pies to meatloaves to crocks of stew. "I wonder if they think I can really eat all this . . . or any of it." He shook his head, and we retreated into the parlor.

"It must be reassuring to know you have so many friends," I said. "They're just trying to be helpful."

Bannerman nodded and reached for a brandy bottle—a bottle he had obviously reached for a number of times that evening. "Damn, Robert." Bannerman poured a glass and then stood listlessly with it in his hand, gazing off into space. "What am I going to do?"

I couldn't think of anything to say, so remained silent.

"This great big house." He shook his head slightly and closed his eyes. "You know, when the children were home, it never seemed like we had quite enough space. We even thought of adding on. Even after they were gone, with just Janey and me, there was never enough room. Now I feel like an old stone in the bottom of a big bucket. Just rattling around." He took a long drink. "It's hard to believe she's really gone." He turned around and saw that there was no glass in my hand. "You'll have to excuse my manners. You want some? Course you do."

"Maybe you'd rather be alone."

"No, of course not. And I don't want to get drunk alone." He smiled slightly and filled a generous portion for me. As he was refilling his own glass, he said, "What's your next move, Robert?"

I shrugged. "First light, I need to ride out to the Staples place. Tom Smith says that's where the other five cattle were headed."

The mention of cattle, and all the memories that word dredged up, brought a look of pain to John Bannerman's face, and he quickly covered it by raising his glass to his lips, swallowing with difficulty.

"You want some company going out there." He said it as a statement, not a question.

"I'd appreciate that, if you can get away, and if you feel like it."

"Christ. Feel like it. I don't feel like anything. I feel hollowed out." He flourished the glass, again half empty. I could see I was going to have to knuckle down and do some serious imbibing if I was to keep pace with him. "That's what this stuff is good for, filling hollows." He reached out a hand. "You got any of those cigars you always got stuck in your mouth?"

"Sure." We both lighted up, and the room soon was blue with sweet-smelling smoke.

"You know what's going to be the hardest, Robert?"

"What's that?"

"Going over to that goddamned bank every day, like nothing has changed, and then having to come home every goddamned night to this empty house. That's going to be hardest, Robert."

"I wish there was something . . ."

Bannerman shook his head violently. "Damn it, don't you start that." He fixed me with a baleful expression, eyes bloodshot. "You know how many goddamn times I've heard that today? Too many." He blew out a thin stream of cigar smoke and coughed, spilling a little of the brandy on the expensive rug at his feet. "Twenty-seven years, Robert. That's how long Janey and I were together. Twenty-seven goddamn good years, too. How old are you?"

"Twenty-nine."

"That's right. You told me that once." He looked puzzled. The brandy was pickling his grief better than any medicine I could have prescribed. "Weren't . . . I thought you said you were only twenty-eight?"

I smiled. "Maybe that was last year."

The brandy glasses were filled again. "Yes," Bannerman said seriously. I couldn't tell if he was joking or not.
"That would make sense." He looked at me, brow furrowed. "What was I talking about?"

"You were married twenty-seven years, and I'm
twenty-nine."

"Right. You realize you were only two goddamn years
old when Janey and me got married?" I nodded. "Pittsburgh. That's where we were married. Did you know I
was from Pittsburgh?" I nodded. "You did? When did I
tell you that?"

"Once upon a time."

"Hmm. We moved to St. Louis and then John Junior
was born, then we moved to Denver and then Teddy was
born. Then we moved to this goddamned town. Bought
the bank, what there was of it then. Twelve years ago
this Christmas."

"That's a lot of territory."

"Damn right. You know that John's a goddamned major now? Never thought he'd make it. God, what a little
pisser he was. More trouble than any ten normal children. A major. A twenty-six-year-old goddamn major.
What do you think about that?"

"He'll be a general by the time he's thirty."

"You bet." Bannerman filled his glass again, then
slopped some in mine. "Or admiral, maybe."

"They don't have admirals in the army, John."

Bannerman didn't respond to that remark but stared
off into space again. "Teddy's the one that's going to be a
rich man, Robert. Twenty-five years old and he's a goddamned lawyer. In New York. You know what I think of
New York?" He made a sound like breaking wind.
"That's what I think of New York. But there's money

there for a young man, Robert. You know," and he leaned forward, his voice confidential. Drunk, but confidential. He reached out a hand and tapped a stubby finger on my knee. "You ought to get yourself out of this one-horse town and make yourself some money. Set up practice in someplace like New York . . . or hell, Chicago or St. Louis. Milk some of those rich bastards, Robert."

"No thanks."

"Why the hell not? You're ambitious, aren't you?"

"Ambition has nothing to do with it."

"Then what the hell does?"

"Why aren't you with some big bank in some big city, doing the same?"

Bannerman sat back and dismissed my question with a belch. "Maybe you're right," he said. "Goddamn, Robert, what am I going to do?" he said again and leaned forward as if he had a cramp, holding his brandy glass in both hands, between his knees.

"You're going to go . . . going to go with me to the Stiples . . . Staples . . . tomorrow. If we're both sober enough to ride."

Bannerman brightened and looked up. "Goddamn right."

"Nobody will miss you at . . . the bank?" The brandy was gaining noticeable control over my tongue, and I resolved that I would nurse this last portion and take no more.

"Miss me?" Bannerman laughed loudly, throwing his head back with mirth. "Robert, I own the goddamn thing. I guess they can do without me. Maybe forever. Do 'em good. Hell, they got some bad habits, Robert. Ever notice that?" He belched. "Wait for my say so before they blow their goddamn noses. 'Mr. Bannerman this, Mr. Bannerman that.' You know what I'd like to do?" He leaned forward again, eyes trying their best to focus on my face. "I'd like to walk into that goddamned bank tomorrow, stand in the middle of the floor, and yell as loud as I goddamn well could, 'Mr. Bannerman's got a first name, by God!' "

"It's jush . . . just respect, John."

"Respect, hell." He lapsed back into his chair, morose. "Pillar of the community."

"What?"

"That's what you and me are. Goddamn pillars of this community."

"Drunk pillars."

Somehow those bloodshot, bleary eyes of his managed a twinkle. "Don't you know too much . . ." and he took the word slowly, working his tongue around all the circular sounds, "alcohol is bad for your health? And you . . . you're a . . . goddamned doctor, too."

"Feel better, don't you?"

"I think I feel worse."

"Different kind of worse, then."

Bannerman nodded and looked like he was going to pass out right there in the chair. He leaned forward, hanging his head, the now empty glass in danger of falling from his grasp.

"Maybe you've had enough. Maybe some sleep . . ."

Bannerman sat bolt upright, frowning at me. He turned slowly and fastened his gaze on the brandy bottle at his elbow, sitting serenely on the small, delicately inlaid table by his chair. "Lookit there," he said. "Still some left, goddamn it." He reached over and grabbed the bottle, but it spun out of his hand. Dizzy with the sudden effort, I stood up and managed the bottle, turning it upright before the brandy sloshed on the fancy table. "Let's finish it, Robert." I poured the remainder in his glass, and he looked up at me. "You aren't having any more?"

"I still got some," I said, and Bannerman's blurred vision looked at my glass. He nodded. It was empty, but he couldn't see that.

He held his own glass near his nose, ready to drink, then lowered it. "Tomorrow, Robert."

"Tomorrow. We'll ride out to the Staples."

Bannerman shook his head. "That first." He struggled for control of his voice, now shaking. "Then we're going to get the bastard that killed my Janey." His eyes came up to meet mine. "They're not going to get away, Robert."

I nodded dumbly. "I talked to McCuskar. He won't be much help."

Bannerman coughed and held a hand up to his mouth. "That's to be expected," he said thickly.

"I thought maybe he'd want to earn his salary," I said.

Bannerman closed his eyes. He wanted to think straight then, but he was too far gone. He shook his head as if to clear it. "If they were still in town," he managed, "then Vince'd be the first person I'd go to." He looked at me, eyes clearly unfocused. "But he isn't . . . I mean they . . . they're not here anymore."

"Maybe we should see the sheriff, then. Ride on over to Coldwater." That seemed like a good idea, so I repeated the suggestion, hoping it would sink in.

Bannerman nodded solemnly. "That's what we'll do. What'd you say his name was?"

"The sheriff?"

The banker looked at me strangely. "No," he said slowly. "Brown, that's it. Mr. Brown. That's the bastard." He downed what little was left of his brandy and slapped the glass down on the table. I winced. "You said he knew the cattle were sick?"

"I think he did, yes."

"Then he murdered my Janey, Robert. Goddamned sick mind to do something like that."

I nodded.

"Well, Mr. Brown, your days are numbered. If it's the last goddamn thing I do. Your goddamn days are numbered, sonny boy." Bannerman finished his speech and tried to stand up, but his knees failed.

"Help me to that goddamned divan," he mumbled, and I did so, noticing again what a large man John Bannerman was. His grip on my arm was like a vise cranked tight, and he made it to the divan before he passed out. I found a shawl and covered him with it. I turned out the kerosene lantern, leaving the house inky, and with the greatest of care made my way to the front door, letting myself out into the stillness of that August night.

It must have been nearly three in the morning. The air felt intoxicating after the smoke and brandy, and I managed a somewhat meandering line back to my office and home. Even though his mind had been fogged with the drink, I knew John Bannerman was deadly serious about the mysterious Mr. Brown.

I wanted to find him almost as badly as Bannerman did, but the thought of the two of us on a manhunt made the hair stand up on my neck. I struggled at my front door. The skeleton key was too large for the hole in the lock. Either the hole expanded or the key finally shrank some, because in due course I was inside and worried.

If the sheriff couldn't help, then what? I was no lawman. Neither was John Bannerman. How would we find Brown? Where had he headed? The two of us wouldn't make much of a threatening posse . . . a young, inexperienced, and drunken physician and a fifty-one-year-old drunken bank president. In the morning neither one of us would be drunk, but that was the only thing that would change.

I struggled upstairs, too tired to undress. I flopped down on the bed. John Bannerman. Dr. Robert N. Patterson. And now, Mr. Brown, do you have a first name too? For the first time in my life I wanted professional help, and not of the medical kind. Sheriff, I thought, you've got to listen to us. And then I passed out.

CHAPTER 8

Considering our conditions, John Bannerman and I almost managed an early start the next morning. I awoke shortly after five, feeling vile and surly with only two hours of heavy, drugged sleep. I awoke sweating, feeling as if I had the entire hide of a steer in my mouth. But I awoke without a headache and was thankful for that.

It was the smell of wood smoke that startled me to wakefulness, I think. It wasn't the good clean smell of a morning breakfast fire, though, and I stumbled out of bed and went to the back window. I could see the fire jetting up to the still dark heavens from about the spot where Sandy Bascomb's cabin had once stood, up on the hill, nearly a half mile away. The wind was gentle, washing down the hill, and it was that breeze that brought the odor of smoke to my nostrils.

Ruben Blumenthal had been true to his word. And being the sensitive soul that he was, he had torched the cabin, presumably occupant and all, before the town was stirring, making sure that the folks who liked to come and gawk were denied a show.

"The poor bastard," I said and turned to make my own preparations. I packed a small roll of provisions, without knowing really what to take, and some bedding. Even with the two years of army life, I was still not expert at that chore, and my saddle roll, the outside layer an old army blanket, was far larger than it needed to be. It looked as if a child had done the job. Muttering with exasperation, I tried again and the second time succeeded in producing a bundle that might not be laughed at by someone polite. That done, I rummaged around and fixed myself some breakfast—two thick slices of bread a day or so too old and a thick slather of marmalade. I had no inclination to start a fire, so I did without coffee.

As a last step, and more out of habit than anything else, I packed my medical bag as well and felt less naked. Fed and packed, I tucked the bedroll under my arm and made for the livery stable. Earl Baines was up before the birds, as usual, and he greeted me cheerfully. And then he nodded up the hill toward where the sparks from Bascomb's shack still rolled up to the sky.

"Hell of a thing, eh, Doc."

"Yes," I said. "I hope that's the end of it."

"Looks like you're headed out," he observed.

"Uh-huh. How's Clara?"

"Fine and dandy," Earl said. "Where you bound so early, anyways?"

"Staples place, then Coldwater," I said and moved past him, in no mood for chatter.

"You want I should saddle her up for you?"

I didn't answer right off but took a moment or two, in the dim light of one dust-covered, cobwebbed lantern, to inspect the mare. Her gums were clear, but she was in no mood to have her mouth inspected. She jerked her head and muttered something, blowing air in my face through wet nostrils.

"Hold still, dammit."

Her eyes were bright and eager, and there were no swellings anywhere on her slick coat. As I moved my hands down her flank, one hind leg seemed just a little too eager to come off the floor of the stall, and I thumped her stoutly.

"Put that hoof down!" I snapped and thumped her again with the flat of my hand. Baines snickered, and the hoof went back on the floor but with no weight on it.

"She's been in that stall too long," Baines observed.

I felt down the tensed leg, and it was clear of any blemishes. "One day? You think that's too long?" I asked.

Behind me, Baines shrugged. "She thinks so."

"Well, she can just unthink so."

"She's always had that habit, you know, Doc."

"Uh-huh. That's a habit I don't have much use for." I had never relished being on the receiving end of a horse's hoof and had often wondered why an animal like my horse, steady-tempered and all, took such a delight in making threats. She had never actually kicked me or anyone else, but the sight of that big hind leg, all bunched up with the hoof poised a few inches off the ground, was enough to give anyone pause.

"She seems sound enough, Earl. Do me a favor and go ahead and get her ready, if you would."

"You want her to have some oats?"

"Sure. Unless she kicks you. Then take the bucket and wrap it over her head."

Baines chuckled again, and I left the livery, rubbing my hands on my trousers to get off the horsey smell. I walked up the street to the Smiths', because Marion had carried out her threat. She had taken her husband home. She was up, clattering about the kitchen of their restaurant, preparing for the customers who might still have confidence in the Branding Iron for breakfast.

"How's Thomas?" I asked.

"He'll do," Marion said in her own clipped way, then her face softened some. "He wanted to be up and around this morning, but I said no. So soon afterward didn't seem like a good idea to me."

"Indeed not. I'd like to look in on him, if that's all right."

"Certainly it's all right," Marion said. She dabbed at a pot of boiling potatoes, then laid the wooden spoon down. "I'll take you up."

I didn't spend much time with the morose Thomas Smith, just long enough to make sure that my work of only hours before had done some good. He had only a slight fever, but I had expected that. The wounds from the surgery, seven pockets gouged into his flesh, looked as good as could be expected. He was half in and half out of sleep, and I didn't linger.

Downstairs again, I turned to Marion. "Listen, Marion, John Bannerman and I will be out of town for a while."

"Staples?"

I nodded.

"Then you should be back by nightfall."

I hesitated. "We're going on over to Coldwater to see Sheriff Edmunds."

"Oh?"

"We might be gone as long as four or five days."

"That's a far ride," she said, eyebrows arching.

"It's the closest sheriff we've got. But if anyone needs anything . . ."

"I'll make sure everyone knows," Marion said, and I was sure that she would. "No one else has come down sick, have they?"

I shook my head. "And I don't think they will. Tom is on the mend, I'm sure of it. I wouldn't go unless it was urgent. I'd like to be able to watch over him for the next forty-eight hours or so, but we really need to go." I didn't say that if the anthrax had gotten into Tom Smith's system there was nothing any doctor could do for him.

"I'm sure I'm capable of caring for him, Doctor." Marion sounded a little stiff, and I couldn't blame her.

"If there is an emergency, you might have someone who's able ride on up to Twin Springs. That's only thirty miles, and there's a doctor there."

"Only thirty miles," Marion said dryly.

"It's the best I can do. We really need to ride to the Staples and find out about those other cattle."

Marion looked me up and down calmly. "Doctor, you don't have to explain yourself to me. You and Mr. Bannerman go on and do what you think you have to do. I'll take care of Thomas. I'm sure folks in this town can keep until you return."

She could see that I was uneasy about dashing off, but she didn't ask why we were seeking out the sheriff. I didn't explain but took my leave as quickly as I could, anxious to see what state of mind John Bannerman was in that morning. It wasn't good.

If he had been drunk the night before, with only a couple hours' sleep, he was a master at concealing the fact. Only the dark shadows under his eyes told the story. He wasn't talking much, but his movements were quick and sure as he completed his own preparation. And I noticed that he rolled a far neater saddle pack than I.

By six o'clock in the morning we were in the saddle, heading for the Staples ranch. Bannerman was mounted on his own classy buckskin gelding, an animal that had spent most of its eight years pulling the Bannerman carriage. The horse didn't look right with a saddle on his back, but I chalked that up to the size of his rider. I thought briefly about making light of John's size on board the animal, but the banker was in no mood for humor. In fact, since we had met moments before, he had muttered only two words, a terse "Good morning."

He was dressed in black, the long coat forking over the cantle of the saddle, and as he eased himself into the saddle, looking like a man afraid he was about to break, I could see that he was wearing a revolver. It was not the small, pearl-handled kind one tends to associate with drawers of a banker's desk.

We rode in silence for the first two or three miles, and it was Bannerman who spoke first. "Where do you figure Brown was headed?" he said quietly.

"I have no idea. I don't even know where the cattle came from. I'm hoping Staples can give us some information about that."

"Tom didn't know?" Bannerman looked at me, eyes dark in the early morning light.

I shook my head. "I'm not a lawman."

"What do you mean by that?"

"I mean I forgot to ask him. And now the carcass is ashes. If there was a brand, it's gone."

"Wonderful, Robert. He didn't have a bill of sale?"

I felt uncomfortable under Bannerman's steady gaze. "I didn't ask to see it. Smith was in no condition to talk after the surgery, and I was in a hurry to get on with it. I didn't ask him beforehand."

Bannerman fell silent, the reins loose in his left hand. "Probably won't tell us much anyway, even if he does have one." He stretched in the stirrups, easing his back. "I've been around cattlemen all my life, one way or another. I'm guessing those cattle were rustled someplace, and as soon as Brown and his partners saw they were sick, they dumped them the easiest and quickest way possible."

"What makes you think so?"

The banker glanced at me again, something close to pity in his dark eyes. "You've lived a sheltered life, my boy. What cattleman pushes only six head? Three men with six head? Doesn't make sense. Of course," and he sighed as he settled back down in the saddle, "rustling only six head doesn't make much sense either, unless you're looking for just a fast buck."

"I wish I knew, John."

After another moment, Bannerman said, "I told Mc-Cuskar we were headed out to the Staples."

"When did you see him?"

"This morning, early. He came by to tell me a bunch of fellows were intent on burning the Bascomb place. Said he wouldn't let them do it until he checked with me first."

"I wouldn't have guessed that he was up so early."

"Maybe he has a guilty conscience," Bannerman said and grinned faintly. "He saw the light on in my kitchen and decided it was safe to bother me."

I grunted. "He wouldn't do anything without making sure he was covered, one way or another."

"That's not altogether true, Robert. He was right to check. No one had told him about Sandy Bascomb or the plans to burn the shack. It happens that I own those buildings. McCuskar wasn't about to take Ruben Blumenthal's word for it."

"You own them?"

"Of course." He said it like I should have known all along. "Anyhow, I told him, and as a matter of course, I filled him in on the situation. He seemed glad you and I were taking care of it. He has no jurisdiction outside the village anyway. He wouldn't be of much help anyway, with the Staples or with . . . Brown."

"You sound like you're planning on running down Brown by yourself, whether the sheriff helps or not."

"That's accurate, Robert." He was looking straight ahead, jaw set.

"You think that's a good idea?"

He looked over at me. "It's just the way it's going to be."

"Neither one of us are lawmen, John. We're not equipped. And at least speaking for myself, I don't know what I'd do if I did catch up with him."

"I know what I'll do." Bannerman's statement was flat, devoid of any emotion.

"Maybe Sheriff Edmunds will take over," I said. "There's been laws broken. I can't see how he can refuse."

"Don't hold your breath, Robert. If we can prove those cattle were stolen, then maybe. And if the sheriff has some idea where to look. Otherwise, Brown can just say he didn't know the animals were sick. If the law catches him, that's all he needs to say. It's his word against anyone else's."

I toyed with the reins as the horses steadily jogged along. "Neither one of us can afford to go chasing around the whole territory, John."

"Speak for yourself," Bannerman said.

Five hours later, we reined the horses in. In front of us stood the Staples place, a small sod house with a scattering of outbuildings and more dogs than I could have ever imagined possible. From the look of the place, Staples was a homesteader, certainly not a cattleman. The only livestock I could see, other than the pack of dogs that yapped at our horses' heels, were a milk cow and a calf, standing stupidly in a small shed just beside the house.

"They must not mind the smell of cow manure in their house," I muttered.

"Better than having to walk through a blizzard to milk her, Robert. Convenience, man."

"A blizzard in August? Not even in this country."

A little tow-headed urchin appeared in the front door and set up a howling that matched the dogs.

"Ma! There's men!" I heard him say, then he darted back inside.

Mrs. Staples was a good-looking woman, even in her drab calico, sun-faded and bleached from who knows how many launderings. Two small faces, one of them the alerting urchin, appeared behind her skirts. Her hair was done up in a severe bun, and her calico dress swelled in the right places, even after giving birth at least twice, but that wasn't what caught my attention. The old Sharps rifle she cradled across her bosom demanded instant respect.

"Morning, ma'am," John Bannerman said, his voice polite and reserved.

"Good morning, gentlemen. Mr. . . . Bannerman, is it?" She smiled, and the rifle lowered a little. Their visits into town were infrequent, but I felt relieved that she recognized my partner. They were a rare family. I had never had occasion to be summoned to their homestead, and they had never paid my office a visit.

"Yes, ma'am. This is Dr. Robert Patterson, from Cooperville also. Robert, this is Alice Staples. And the little ones . . . ah, let me see. Vernon, the one on the right, and ah . . . Todd. Fine young men, both of them." Mrs. Staples beamed with pleasure and turned to set the Sharps behind the door.

"Will you gentlemen come in?" she said. We still hadn't dismounted.

"If it's just the same to you, ma'am, thanks just the same. We need to talk to your husband," I said.

"Is it about the cattle?" Her face was suddenly sober.

"Yes, ma'am, as a matter of fact, it is."

She nodded. It was the first time I had met the family, but already my admiration for them was growing. She was a levelheaded woman. "You'll find him out back. There's a cow path that leads to a copse of trees. That's where the healthy cattle are. You'll find Corey just beyond that, with the sick ones, I think he is."

"Much obliged," Bannerman said, and he tipped his hat to the woman and made a face at Vernon, who piped shrilly and ducked behind the safety of the calico.

Mrs. Staples' "just beyond" turned out to be a considerable ride beyond the copse of trees. There were perhaps a dozen head of cattle there, and they all looked relatively alert and normal.

"If he's got anthraxed cattle out here, you'd best not let your horse graze any," I said. Bannerman nodded. The anthrax was a soil bacillus and would be returned to the soil in the cow manure, making the pasturage lethal for other livestock.

We saw a man in the distance but could see no other cattle. Beside him was a handmade wheelbarrow, and he was working industriously. As we drew nearer, we could see that he was shoveling a light-colored substance into a deep pit before him. He heard the crunch of our horses' hooves on the dry grass and turned quickly. I noticed that he dropped the shovel abruptly and took in hand another tool. The rifle he held, muzzle pointed in our direction, was not an old Sharps. It was a Winchester, holding enough rounds of ammunition to destroy an army. I recognized it. It was much like the one in my own saddle scabbard but of heavier caliber. I had time to reflect on that, because the bore of Staples' rifle winked at me darkly as he shifted it away.

"You'll pardon the reception," Staples said and leaned the rifle against the wheelbarrow.

"Quite all right," Bannerman replied easily. I wasn't sure it was quite all right. My stint in the Army had taught me that there was little of benefit that came roaring out of the end of those things.

"Mr. Bannerman, good day to you. Who might your escort be?"

I swung down from the saddle and extended a hand. "I'm Robert Patterson," I said. Staples held up his gloved hands.

"Another time," he said. I left Clara's reins looped over the saddle horn, and she stood like a statue. Walking to the edge of the pit, I saw the corpses of the five steers, several feet down and already with a liberal coating of lime from Staples' shovel.

"We came to talk with you about the cattle," Bannerman said, leaning forward in his saddle.

"There they are," Staples replied, gesturing with contempt at the pit. "I sure got sweet-talked into that deal, I can tell you that."

"You know what was wrong with them?" I asked.

"Hell, yes, I know. Didn't know when I bought them. Thought they were just trail-weary." He snorted. "Trail-weary with anthrax. Don't take a genius to recognize that."

"Dr. Patterson here is from Cooperville too," Bannerman said. "We had an outbreak of anthrax there. Came from a steer that a restaurant owner purchased. We need to track down the owners of that stock, Mr. Staples. Thought maybe you could help us some."

"If I could help, I'd be more than obliged."

"You have a bill of sale for them?"

"Of course. I got it tucked away in the house. I was sort of hoping Mr. Burns would come this way again." He looked at the Winchester pensively. "Maybe he'd make good."

"Was the brand of origin on the bill?"

"Yes, it was."

"And it matched the brand running on the hoof?" Bannerman asked. He was standing near the pit, but we couldn't see any marks on the covered hides below us.

"Well, of course. I'd check a thing like that, no matter who I bought stock from."

Bannerman looked at Staples. "I know many a man who wouldn't bother."

"Well, it seemed like kind of a small operation, sellin' one in town, then comin' out here on someone's suggestion," Staples said. "Burns said he'd sold one in town, but he said they'd come up from the south. Thought maybe he meant Willow Creek."

"No, it was Cooperville. He introduced himself to you as Burns?"

"Uh-huh. The one that did the talkin'. Had two men with him that stayed with the cattle. He came right into the house. Fed him coffee, even."

"What'd he look like?"

Staples' description labeled the man we knew as Brown. I asked, "How long after the men left did the cattle go before they came up sick?"

Staples pushed his hat brim up with the back of his glove, brow furrowed in thought. "Two days until one went down and wouldn't get up. But they was sick the day after. I thought maybe it was colic, from travelin' too much. But then, the one went down, and I got a closer look. That's when I knowed."

"How did you get them out here?" I asked.

"Drug the one that was down, after I shot her. Herded the rest. They sure didn't want to move much. I penned 'em up here and dug the hole. Then I shot 'em. All five. Gone just like that."

"You did the right thing, if that's any consolation," Bannerman said.

"Did you mix them in with any of your other stock?"

Staples shook his head. "Sure didn't. Glad now, I didn't. Bad enough to lose fifty dollar. I was just too eager, I guess. Seemed like a good price, delivered right to the door. Weren't such a bargain, was it?" Staples smiled wryly.

"You know you shouldn't run your cattle on this pasture, then?"

"Yeah, I know it. I'll fence out this part, though Lord knows where the money will come from for that."

Bannerman scuffed an expensive boot in the dust, then looked at Staples. "You need money for the winter, you come and see me."

"Thanks, but I'd just as soon not be owin' more than I do right now."

The banker nodded but didn't press the issue.

"You a doctor, huh?" Staples said, looking at me.

"That's right."

"Any folk take sick from the anthrax? That cook . . . the one who bought the other beef . . . he didn't know?"

"No, he didn't know."

"And no one took sick?"

I hesitated, not wanting to reopen the wound that Bannerman had been so successful at concealing. But the banker beat me to it. When he spoke, his voice was hard and businesslike.

"Two people took sick, Mr. Staples. My wife and another innocent man."

Staples looked quickly at me, then down at the ground. "I'm sorry to hear that, sir." He didn't question further, knowing, I suppose like any other rancher, that the anthrax spared no one.

"The two men that were with Brown, or Burns, as he called himself to you, are dead," I said.

"The anthrax?"

"Yes."

"Then that evens the score just a mite, don't it?" Staples said harshly. "Goddamn them all to hell. Why would a man do a thing like that?"

"That's what we aim to find out," I said. "We'd appreciate looking at the bill of sale now. And I'd like to examine your family. And you too, for that matter. Just as a precaution."

"I'd be much obliged if you would, Doc. I cleaned up the place as best I could. There was a pile of manure in the front yard, before they got moved into pasture. I cleaned that up and buried it too and spread lime in the yard. That's why the young'uns are inside for a spell."

"You're a smart man."

Staples shrugged and dumped the last of the lime in the pit. "You wouldn't a said that a couple days ago," he said bitterly. "Man learns bit by bit. Sometimes slower than others."

We went back to the house, Bannerman and I on horseback and Staples pushing the wheelbarrow. It was nearly a half mile, but he didn't seem to notice. The man had an endless capacity for work.

With the family so far from town, it seemed a good opportunity to be thorough. With some urging from Corey Staples, I examined the entire family, taking one at a time into a small bedroom. Vernon had eyes only for John Bannerman, whose mugging kept him in near hysterics, and the lad tolerated me only long enough to have the ordeal over with. Little Todd, however, giggled and twisted every time I touched him, thinking the examination was the most fun he had had in his days on the lonely prairie. I let him listen to his own heart through the stethoscope, and his eyes got so big I thought they would pop.

The Staples were healthy. I was thankful for that and credited it to Corey's good sense after an initial mistake. When we were ready to leave, I walked away from the house with the man, explaining what I wanted.

"Mr. Staples, you seem aware of anthrax, and you've acted correctly. I think everything will be all right. But if anyone in your family shows signs of a boil, or carbuncle, or whatever you want to call it, you come into town immediately. Don't wait for the next morning or whenever. You come see me, right then. Do you understand?"

"Yup."

"Any time, day or night. You come."

"I hear you, Doc."

"And now I'll be frank with you. Your danger is from breathing the contagion. Handling the hides, that sort of thing."

"I kept my distance."

"Not the first day, you didn't. If you were going to be sick, you probably would have come down with it by now. I could detect no sign when I examined you. But if you should develop a cough, or a tightness in the chest, dizziness, or upset, the best thing for it is to get out of that house. Get away from your family. Come into town and see me, immediately."

"You make it sound like I won't have much choice but to keel over and die," Staples said soberly.

"Once the contagion is inside the body, not simply in the skin, it is invariably fatal. Mr. Bannerman's wife died, so did Sandy Bascomb. So did the two cattlemen. You are essentially correct, Mr. Staples. So you can appreciate my concern for you and your family. As I say, I think the danger is probably past for you, as long as you restrict that pasturage. The lime will have killed the contagion, but there's no way to be sure you've gotten it all."

"You sayin' maybe it would be best to move off this place?"

"Not off the ranch. But to a different location for the house, yes. I'm saying that would be a good idea. Once the anthrax is in the soil, it's there permanently. You can't lime your entire homestead."

Staples stood musing. "There's a line shack up the valley just a short piece, and it's on my land. I guess this house ain't so much that we couldn't fix that up just as good or better. We ain't got just a world of goods." He smiled at me.

"Then I say, do it. The sooner the better."

"I'll think on it," he said, and then Bannerman came out of the house, with Vernon hanging on his coattails. The big banker picked him up and tossed him a good yard in the air, high over his head, to a squeal of delight. Todd looked on happily but content to stay in the shadow of his mother's skirts.

"Thank God they're all healthy," Bannerman said a few moments later as we rode out, the sun hot on our faces. "That's a nice family." And then he lapsed into silence. I could see the pain on his face. The sight of the man and wife and two small boys brought memories that were still too fresh to the surface. We rode across the rugged country toward Coldwater. I felt confident that the anthrax had been halted, at least in my neighborhood. What herd the infected animals came from remained to be answered. The brand on the sales receipt, barely legible, said the animals had been Walking Double S stock. If they were from the area, the brand might be registered in Coldwater, at the courthouse. If not, then at least there was a telegraph there, and we could track down the home ranch . . . home for both the cattle and the anthrax.

And that left only one task ahead of us. The man Brown had more debts to pay. I was sure it was he who occupied John Bannerman's thoughts as we rode east and south.

CHAPTER 9

"Well now, the Double S is no mystery," the clerk said and thumbed through the ledger he had pulled down out of the musty shelves. "I recognize it but don't rightly remember, off the top of my head. But we'll just check."

"Walking Double S," I corrected. We had arrived in Coldwater in midday—a day and a half out of Staples' and bone-weary. Sheriff Max Edmunds was out of town. His deputy tending shop, a friendly but taciturn fellow named Bernie Kidder, assured us that our business could wait until Edmunds returned—the next day or maybe the day after that. I was ready for sleep in a bed instead of a trail roll, but Bannerman was hot on the scent. He wanted to track down the brand and saw daylight as the time to do it. I followed wearily.

"Walking Double S," the clerk announced, waving his hand with a flourish. "Goodness! That's been a registered brand for sixteen years!" I tried to read the inverted ledger, but the clerk's ink-stained fingers were in the way.

"Who?" Bannerman asked, leaning his elbows on the clerk's desk, nearly bent double, trying to read the fine scratching.

The clerk adjusted his glasses. "Samuel L. Burns. I thought I remembered. Sam Burns. Yup. That's the Walking Double S."

"Where's the home ranch?"

The clerk's finger ran across the line and stopped. "Says here, 'Thatcher.' That don't ring any bell, but as I recall, Sam Burns has one hell of a big spread, gents. Near legend. Hell, if I heard of him way down here, he's got to be legend, right?"

"I suppose," I said. Samuel L. Burns. A full name had been supplied, but I had a hunch the rancher Burns was not the same man who had been hoofing the anthraxed cattle all over southern Colorado. John Bannerman must have been thinking the same thing.

"What's this Sam Burns look like?" the banker asked. "You recall?"

The clerk snapped the book shut and thrust it back on the shelf, in company with perhaps fifty others. He scratched his head and then shook it. "Sorry. Can't be of help there. Can't say as I've ever met the gentleman. Heard lots about him and his outfit but never met him." He chuckled. "Last thing I heard was him getting the dander up of the other stockmen."

"How's that?"

"Well," and the clerk strung out the word like he was starting a real whopper of a yarn, "I don't know the details, and it's been a year or two. But old Sam, he don't think much of overloading his range. All the other boys wanted to hold stock 'till late, don't you know, to help drive the prices up. Sam thought that was ridiculous, and he drove anyways, early in the fall. Took near five thousand head to the rail yards. The others hung on, cussing him a blue streak. Then we got one of those freak winters. Freak, hell, seems we get 'em every year. But anyways, we had an early snow. You boys remember, I'm sure. Turned into a real pisser. To make a long story short, a whole passel of ranchers ended up losing a fair number of cattle. Winter came so hard and so early, they couldn't drive, early, late, or any other way. They lost, and old Sam Burns sat back on his pile of money, feelin' pretty smug, I'd guess. Didn't go over so good with his neighbors, I'm told."

Bannerman looked at me and raised an eyebrow. He turned and thumped the desk. "Sir, we thank you for your trouble."

"No trouble. That's what I'm here for," the clerk said and smiled as Bannerman and I left his office.

When we were out in the street of Coldwater, Bannerman said, "The Sam Burns that clerk was talking about isn't the man we're after. A man who runs cattle in the thousands, and is that shrewd about his range and the weather, isn't going to waste time driving a half-dozen sick cattle all over hell's half acre."

I nodded. "You know, Edmunds is going to have a hard time finding Brown, or Burns, or whatever his name is. He didn't exactly leave a smoking trail for anyone to follow."

"He'll be in the area."

I looked at the banker with surprise. "How do you know that?"

"With as easy pickings as he's had, he'd be crazy not to. Let's assume Brown rustled the cattle from the Burns ranch. That might explain why he used Burns's name on the sales papers he gave young Staples. Who'd ever know, unless Staples crossed tracks with Burns himself, which is unlikely. My guess is that Brown will head back in the general direction of the Walking Double S."

"Maybe."

"Right now, let's hunt us up an artist."

"A what?"

"An artist. Somebody that's good at drawing pictures. Like of people. Like of Brown. You remember him well enough?"

"Couldn't forget him."

"Then we'll get a picture to show people."

"We? I thought the whole purpose of coming here was to get Max Edmunds to do the looking."

"Like I said, don't hold your breath," Bannerman said. It occurred to me that I was now following John Bannerman, and it didn't take much to see that he was fixed on tracking down the man who had killed his wife. Edmunds might offer help, but I had the impression then that it wouldn't matter to Bannerman one way or the other what the sheriff said.

Bannerman pointed quickly and stepped out into the street, angling across toward a saloon.

"Best place to find out about things," he said.

We entered the Diamond Stud, and because it was midday or after, and in the middle of the week, the place was quiet, with only a couple of men playing cards in the back at a table, and one other man at the bar, a mug of beer in front of him.

The bartender was burly and bearded, looking like he would have no trouble in clearing out trouble from his establishment should the need arise. He glanced at me, and then at John Bannerman, and his gaze took in the measure of the banker. Indeed, in the black frock coat with the black derby, John Bannerman was impressive. I could have won some money having folks try to guess his occupation. No one would have come close.

"Gentlemen, welcome to Coldwater." I hadn't realized the two of us were such obvious newcomers.

"Thank you, sir," Bannerman said affably and leaned

against the bar, looking trail-weary. "If you've got a cold ale, I'd appreciate it." He turned to me. "Robert?"

I nodded, and the bartender quickly and efficiently filled two mugs and slid them onto the bar in front of us. Bannerman paid for both and took a deep swallow, sighing as the brew slid down his dusty throat. At least that was the impression he gave the bartender. We had stopped at another saloon before visiting the clerk, and I knew Bannerman was not as thirsty as he seemed.

"Say," Bannerman said, setting the mug down and beckoning the bartender. "You might be able to help some. You know anyone in Coldwater that can draw a pretty fair portrait?"

The man looked quizzical. "Portrait?"

"Yes. You know, a picture of someone. I'd like to have a picture done. A portrait. Nothing complicated. I'm not looking for a Gilbert Stuart."

"Who's he?" the bartender asked.

"A painter. Did Washington, among others. But as I say, I'm not that particular."

The bartender looked at Bannerman, and I could tell he was deciding that Bannerman *was* someone. He looked a little more interested.

Bannerman, ever skillful with words, had lent the impression that he wanted a portrait of himself, and the bartender didn't ask any more questions.

"Hmm," he said, thinking hard. Then his wide hairy face lit up. "Now say, the man you ought to talk to is Geoffrey Dana." The bartender made that pronouncement and then stood, a smile on his face like we should know this Dana fellow.

"Dana?" Bannerman said.

"Geoffrey Dana. Editor of the Coldwater *Weekly Enterprise.*"

"Ah, a newspaperman."

"Yes, indeed. Comes in here from time to time. Can hold his liquor with the best of 'em."

"And you say he's an artist?"

The bartender shrugged. "Well now, as close to as you're going to find. Does his own engravings, some of the time, and some of them raise an eyebrow. If he can't do for you, then he sure could tell you who might."

"Where might we find this fellow?" I asked.

"Right down the street, come to the intersection, and turn left. Second building on your left after that. Says *Enterprise* over the door, big as life."

"What say we try that, Robert?" Bannerman said and drained his beer. "Your name, sir?"

The bartender smiled and extended a remarkably clean hand. "Fats Dickson," he said and pumped Bannerman's hand.

"Well, Mr. Dickson, you've been a help. I'm sure we'll be seeing you again."

The *Weekly Enterprise* was indeed easy to find, and Geoffrey Dana was industriously at work, not at writing, not at artistry, not with presswork. He was up to his elbows in a complex machine, with half of its parts spread over a low worktable. We waited patiently at the rail that separated the front part of his office from the printing area, and in due course he left the machine and came forward, wiping his hands on a dirty rag. He didn't offer to shake hands.

"What's that you're working on?" Bannerman asked.

"That is what's left of a typewriter," Dana said, looking over his shoulder with an expression of acute distaste.

"It's supposed to be faster than a pencil. It might be, if it worked. I saw an advertisement for it and ordered it, and there it is. Biggest pile of damned junk ever invented. Whoever invented it will die in the poorhouse, if I have anything to say about it."

"I've heard of them," Bannerman said with interest.

"I'm sure you two boys didn't come to talk about my machinery," Dana said and leaned on the railing, cloth in hand. "What can I do for you."

"I assume you're Geoffrey Dana," Bannerman said.

"The one and only."

"Name's Bannerman. John Bannerman. This is Dr. Robert Patterson. We're from over west, from Cooperville."

"Long ride."

"Indeed it is. Fats Dickson says you can draw a mean picture."

Dana smiled and stood up straight, tossing the rag into a corner. "Dickson said that, eh? Well, he's right. I can. When I have the time." He nudged a small pile of papers near my elbow. "Have a look in there, and judge for yourself."

I leafed through the most recent copy of the *Weekly Enterprise*. It was a neat, clean publication, no tent journal.

"We were wondering if you could do a portrait for us," I said.

"For the paper? You boys do something newsworthy?"

"No," I said, "hardly that. We need a portrait of a man we're hunting. Something to show to people."

"Oh. You lawmen?" Then he remembered the introductions. "No, you're a doctor." He looked at Bannerman. "You with the law?"

"No. I'm president of the Bank of Cooperville."

"Fancy that. Well, gents, despite appearances, I'm not a man with a whole world of time on my hands. Unless there's a real good reason, I'll have to turn you down."

"The man we're seeking," Bannerman said, "is responsible for the deaths of at least four people. He's been driving sick cattle around the range. We need to find him and stop him, before anyone else gets hurt."

Dana looked interested, and he pulled a pipe out of his shirt pocket, taking great care with its loading. "So you want something like a wanted poster, is that right?"

"Exactly."

"Max Edmunds know about all this?"

"He will, when he comes back into town."

Dana struck a large match and applied it to his pipe, looking through the smoke first at Bannerman, then me. "You know," he said, whipping out the match, "there's been some trouble with the antics of vigilantes in these parts."

"So?"

"So you two seem like respectable gentlemen to me, and if there's something I can do to bring to justice the vermin that make life miserable for the rest of us, I'm glad to do it. But . . ." He paused and struck another match. "You say Max Edmunds will know. If he says it's the thing to do, I'll help you out. Otherwise, no."

"You're a cautious man, Mr. Dana."

"And I still have a newspaper office and the respect of this community. I don't know you gentlemen from Adam."

"We'll make it worth your time."

"You will, if I do it. First I talk with the sheriff. I'm not a man to waste my time."

"Would you consider doing the picture and holding it for Edmunds' say so? To save time?"

Dana thought that over for a moment, again taking time to gaze at the two of us, his gray eyes methodically collecting and sifting information.

"I guess there's nothing wrong with that," he said at last.

"I'll tell you what the man looks like, and you go from there," I said eagerly.

"Hold on there, young man," Dana said. "I've got a busy afternoon ahead of me. What say you gents come back this evening, say around eight? Then we can work on this thing in peace and quiet."

I groaned inwardly. Lord, how I wanted to be in bed. My eagerness was flagging, but Bannerman didn't let up. "You've got yourself a deal," he said. He looked at me. I nodded, too tired to argue.

"It will be worth your time, Mr. Dana," Bannerman said.

I don't remember what time we finished with Dana that night. I do remember my first impressions of Max Edmunds when we met him the next afternoon. He had been a lawman for nearly as many years as my lifetime, and every trail he had followed, every miserable day he had spent chasing desperadoes and maintaining law and order, showed in his lined face.

He was as tall as me, and probably weighed about the same, but there the similarity ended. His hands were gnarled, and the muscles of his lower arms, visible below his rolled-up sleeves, were like cords of tough rope. His black hair was liberally flecked with gray, and his eyes were such a deep shade of brown that they appeared almost black in some lights. He was tired and trying his best to be civil with us. The deputy sat quietly in a corner, feet up on the corner of a shaky table, while Edmunds heard us out.

"You have any idea how much rustling goes on in this country?" he said finally. His voice was oddly thin and high-pitched.

"Too much," John Bannerman said, feeling much more at ease with the sheriff than I. They were almost the same age, and Edmunds seemed to direct most of his questions at the banker rather than at me. "But the rustling is only a minor part of it."

"Rustling ain't minor," Edmunds snapped.

"Let me finish, if you would," Bannerman said calmly. "Minor compared to what happened afterward."

"You say how many died from the anthrax?"

"Four, at least," I answered.

"And you say this fellow Brown, or whoever he is, knew that the cattle were sick? Even before he disposed of them?"

"That's what one of his partners said before he died."

"You heard him say that."

"Yes."

"He could have meant somebody else, you know."

"I doubt that."

"Why?"

I shrugged. "There's no reason to think so is all."

"How come Brown didn't catch the anthrax too?"

"Heaven only knows. He must have been more careful than the others."

"I guess. Seems pretty farfetched to me."

"There's four dead, including my wife, that says differently," Bannerman said. "He found out the cattle were sick and dumped them on innocent people, just as quick as he could. That makes him guilty of murder."

Edmunds looked at Bannerman, eyes squinting. "Maybe," he said. He picked up the sales receipt Bannerman had taken from Staples and looked at it for the tenth time. "If . . . well, hell, I know the answer to that already. Sam Burns isn't involved in this. Might have some sick cattle, but this isn't something he'd do. He's honest as the day is long." Edmunds' eyes flicked to me briefly. "You'd know this Brown if you ever saw him again?"

"Of course. I spent the better part of half a day with him. Geoffrey Dana said he'd draw up a picture of him if you said it was all right." I didn't say that Dana had already completed the sketch, a remarkable likeness of the man we hunted.

"That'd help. Still don't know what we can do other than keep our eyes open. Might have Dana print up some copies of that picture and post 'em here and there." He settled back in his chair and looked over at the silent deputy. "What you think, Bernie?"

The deputy's feet came down from the table. "Might not hurt to scout around up in Burns's neck of the woods."

"Why don't you do that, then. Leave first light. Ride on up and have a chat with Burns." Edmunds stood up, stretching, one hand at the small of his back. "You two gentlemen need to write out a deposition for me and sign it. I appreciate your riding over here. Can't promise you any satisfaction, but then, you never know what's going to turn up."

"We'd like to ride with the deputy," John Bannerman said flatly.

Edmunds stopped in midstretch and stared at Bannerman. "Don't be ridiculous."

"I don't call it ridiculous," the banker said softly.

"Well, that's what I call it," Edmunds snapped. "This is a job for the law."

"I don't guess I need no help," Bernie said.

"I've got a stake in this," Bannerman persisted. He leaned forward and stabbed a thick forefinger at the sheriff. "You have two choices. We can ride with your deputy, a posse, if you want to call it that. Or we'll just follow along behind. We're going, one way or another."

Edmunds' eyes flashed. "Don't you talk about what choices I have, mister. You interfere with the law and you'll answer to me."

Their eyes locked for several seconds. Bannerman saw he could not bully the man into seeing his way and tried another tack. "How many deputies you got, Sheriff?"

"Three."

"And those three men, and yourself, cover all this territory?"

"We do."

"And you're objecting to help from a couple fit civilians? Sheriff, we know the man you're hunting. Doc here would recognize him a mile away. Now a drawing is fine, but that's not the same."

"I don't want you in the way. If this fella Brown has done all you say he has, then he's not just another punk rustler out for an easy dollar. There comes a fight, I doubt that you two gents are exactly Bernie's first choice for help."

"I'm not exactly a has-been," Bannerman said, standing up. He swung back his coat and pulled the large revolver out of its scabbard with one deft movement, slamming it down sideways on Edmunds' desk. "Now I've carried that, off and on, for fifteen years. A Colt's .44 Navy before that. I can ride, I can shoot, and I take some pride in being able to think straight in most circumstances. If I can't keep up, I'll willingly turn back."

"Put that gun away, Mr. Bannerman," Edmunds said. He looked at me. "What do you think about all this, Doctor? You've been rather quiet."

I had been quiet. It had never been my intent to go off into the prairie, looking for a killer. I had intended to lay the matter in Edmunds' lap and let justice be done—by Edmunds or his deputies.

"I was in the Army for two years, sheriff. The trail is not exactly a foreign place to me, either."

"Rank?"

"I was a lieutenant."

"Medical corps?"

"Well, yes."

"Hardly the same thing, is it?"

"No, I suppose it's not."

"I've hunted with Robert," Bannerman said, pressing. "He can handle himself."

"I'm sure of that. And if you get yourself killed, Doctor, where does that leave Cooperville?"

"There are other doctors. And I'm not planning on getting killed."

"One never does," Edmunds said and sat back down. He laced his fingers together and held them in front of his mouth, staring at his desktop.

"Bernie?"

The deputy shrugged. "I guess I'd rather have 'em up where I could keep an eye on 'em than doggin' my tracks. Either one of you any good at trail cookin'?"

"I can manage," Bannerman said.

"Then hell, let 'em go, Sheriff. You know my cookin'."

Edmunds sighed. "Bernie has a somewhat different outlook on life than most of us," he said dryly and came as close to smiling as I think he ever did. "I'll tell you what. Ride along, if you want. That man," and he pointed at Bernie, "is the boss. He is the law, gentlemen, a duly sworn deputy. If he asks you for assistance, you may render it, using your own good judgment. He even has the power to deputize you, if he thinks that is necessary." He looked first at Bannerman and then me. "Don't get in his way. He knows his job."

"That's all we ask," Bannerman said. "We thank you."

"I can't imagine I've done you any favor," Edmunds said. "Bernie, why don't you get yourself over to Dana's and get him working on that picture of Brown."

"He's got it all ready," I said, and Edmunds shot me a glare.

"You said he was going to do it," the sheriff said quietly.

"We had him work on it yesterday, as long as you were out of town. Didn't want to waste any time."

"Go get it, Bernie." The deputy left and then Edmunds said, "Any more surprises?"

"No."

Edmunds finally let his eyes drop, and he pulled a piece of paper and a pencil out of his desk. "Write me up a short description of everything you told me while we're waiting for the picture. I'll keep it for my files. Might be the possibility that two gents as impulsive as you won't be around for any trial that might come our way."

I almost had the deposition finished, with John Bannerman's help, when the deputy returned. He had a piece of stiff paper in hand, carefully rolled up.

"Sheriff, look who we got here," he said and handed the picture to Edmunds, who unrolled it and regarded it with a critical eye.

"Well, I'll be goddamned," he said. "Your description didn't place with me, Doc, but this here sure does. There's no question this is the man you spent time with?"

"No question at all," I replied, thinking that Dana had done a faithful job of reproducing Brown's general appearance. "You know him?"

Edmunds laughed humorlessly and put the drawing down. He rummaged through the papers on his desk and finally found the one he wanted. He handed the poster to Bannerman. "You could have saved Dana some time," he said. " 'Cept his picture is a good deal better."

Bannerman handed the wanted poster to me, and the familiar face stared up at me. "Aloysius Blaine," I said, reading the name.

"Or Brown, or any number of other names he cares to invent at the spur of the moment," Edmunds remarked.

"Who did he kill?"

"Murdered a woman south of here, in Bayard. They say he just showed up one morning when the husband was away, shot the lady, and ransacked the house. Made off with a little over nineteen dollars." Edmunds must have seen me turn pale. "You're a lucky man, Doc. I'm surprised he didn't just shoot you on the spot and take what few cents you had."

"Loyal to his partners," I said.

"Ha," Edmunds laughed. "Blaine isn't loyal to anyone,

except Blaine. You just caught him in a good mood." He
took the poster back. "Bernie, now you got an idea of
what to do."

"Yep."

"You have some idea where this Blaine tends to hole
up?" Bannerman asked.

"No," Edmunds said flatly, "but we know a couple
things about him. He's never been in my territory before, so I haven't had the pleasure of shooting the son of a
bitch. He usually works alone. Your story about him being hitched up with two other men kind of surprises me.
Them two would have died sooner or later is my guess, if
not from the anthrax, then from Blaine's gun. And he's a
worthless bastard. Killing a woman for nineteen dollars
ought to give you some kind of idea. Sell six dead-on-the-
hoof steers when everyone knows damn well what anthrax can do ought to tell you something else. He likes
the cards, and there's word he's wanted up in Denver for
shooting a faro dealer. He probably hit a losing streak
and dropped fifty cents."

"He sounds sick," I commented.

"Course he's sick. He's a worthless, sick son of a bitch
that the law just hasn't caught up with yet."

"We'll remedy that," Bannerman said softly. There
was such venom in his voice that I looked up quickly.
Edmunds caught the comment too.

"You just keep your shirt on, Mr. Bannerman. I don't
think you have a real notion of just who you're so dead
anxious to meet up with."

"I've got a real good notion," Bannerman said in the
same deadly tone.

"Yeah, maybe you do," Edmunds said. "Maybe you do
at that. Bernie, if I was you, I'd check with Sam Burns

first, like I was sayin'. Kind of get the lay of the land up that way. Show that poster around. Someone may have a line on Blaine that's a little fresher."

"First light," Bernie said to us. He was the picture of confidence, standing there in Edmunds' office, the silver star pulling on his shirt and the heavy Colt .45 jutting from his hip.

"First light," John Bannerman said, now eager. I just nodded, wishing I could share the confidence the two of them so obviously felt.

CHAPTER 10

We didn't have any trouble keeping up with Deputy Bernie Kidder. On his feet, he was an erect young man, perhaps five years younger than me, nearly six feet tall, with unruly blond hair that nearly covered his ears. In the saddle he slouched, back bent in a bow, taking the shocks of the horse's footsteps like a spring. Most of the time he kept the reins of his leggy palomino looped over the saddle horn, so that his hands were free for more important things—like rolling cigarettes. Deputy Kidder, young in years, was an old-timer when it came to cigarette rolling. And it wasn't often when the fresh cigarette was not rolled into his mouth and lighted from the stub of the last one or another one was not in the process of production.

In the rare times when his hands weren't thus employed, he rode with both hands on the horn, covering the loop of reins, as if he was incapable of holding himself up without that support. If his horse had any gait other than a brisk walk, we didn't discover it until late in the afternoon of the second day, when a tall, gangly jackrabbit broke cover in front of us and raced away, ears straight up and hind legs pumping him in a long series of ten-yard leaps. Without a word, Kidder spat out the cigarette butt that was in his mouth and booted the palomino, whose ears were already perked and tracking the rabbit. The horse broke into an instantaneous flat-out gallop, tail streaming and neck pumping with power. My horse startled, but I checked the reins, and Clara remained in a sedate walk, as did Bannerman's buckskin.

Kidder and his mount gained on the rabbit, not by speed but by shortcuts. From the faint trail we watched with wonder as the deputy seemed to think two leaps ahead of the rabbit, closing the gaps by hurtling over hummocks and across shallow water cuts in the prairie.

"That young fellow is plain crazy," Bannerman observed. When the rider closed within twenty yards of the frantic rabbit, an animal who no doubt was surprised in its own rabbit way that it should be losing a race to something as large and ungainly as a horse, I saw Kidder reach down and unholster his revolver. He rode pell-mell, holding the gun in front of him, barrel slightly raised.

He fired in one quick snap, the flat report coming to our ears only after we saw the sand leap behind the rabbit when the bullet struck. The second shot struck the rabbit and sent it rolling and kicking into a scrub bush, and Kidder pulled his horse to a trot, riding up to the bush and stopping. He looked down for a minute and then rode back toward us, angling across the prairie, the palomino once more in a steady walk, blowing hard.

"I wouldn't have thought that possible with a six-gun," I observed. Kidder joined us, his face split in a wide grin. He was shucking the two spent shell casings out of the Colt and drew two fresh rounds from his belt.

"Not a rabbit on the range is safe," Bannerman said to the deputy.

"Nope."

"You must practice a good deal."

Kidder nodded. "You get so you can do that to a runnin' rabbit, then a man ain't much problem." It was the first time he had mentioned the purpose of the trip in two days of riding. He had talked about everything else but that. He finished reloading the revolver and snapped the gate closed, holstering the weapon. And then he rolled himself a long-overdue cigarette.

After it was lighted, he said, "I figure we're about ten mile from Burns's place, give or take. We'll be seein' some of his stock any time now, about when we see the river."

A half hour later we saw nearly a hundred head of cattle, mashing down the banks of the Apishapa River and muddying the water as they drank. Kidder rode up near a group of five steers, leaning from his saddle.

"Walkin' Double S," he announced, straightened up, and grinned. "We ain't lost, at least."

I looked up at the sun, still a good hand above the horizon. "How far now to the ranch?"

"About five mile, give or take," the deputy said. I nodded. His estimates, despite the "give or takes," were generally proving accurate.

"We'll mosey on in and be there in time for a late supper, maybe," Kidder added. He looked at John Bannerman and grinned. "Nothin' against your beans, Mr. Bannerman, but a bean's a bean, no matter how she's cooked."

It was no more than a good hour when we crested a smooth rise in the prairie and saw the ranch nestled in a copse of cottonwoods. The house was large and well tended, and the barn, a monstrous, flat-roofed affair, set back from the house a hundred yards, a large complex of corrals and cattle chutes filling in the gap between barn and house.

The inevitable dogs saw us and set up a clamor, running to greet us as we walked the horses down the hill toward the house. We were still two hundred yards away when a man came out of the barn. He stood by the double doors, watching us approach, making no move to come out in the open to greet us.

"Afternoon," he said when we rode near enough to hear without his having to raise his voice. His eyes scanned our faces, then came to rest on Kidder's badge, and he seemed to relax some.

"Mr. Burns to home?" Kidder asked, leaning on the saddle horn again like he'd lost his spine.

The man, short, dark, and Spanish, I guessed, nodded. "He is in the house, senor."

"Would you be good enough to tell him he's got three trail-weary visitors?" the deputy said and grinned. Without a word the man unstuck himself from the doorjamb of the barn and limped off toward the house, dragging a right leg that was stiff from hip to ankle. We rode the horses over to where a corner of the corral jutted out into the yard, and mindful of the dogs, swung down to tie the horses. Kidder dusted himself off, and then the three of us, deputy in the lead, walked toward the house.

A small, low, somehow incongruous picket fence bounded a patch of clipped grass around the front of the house, and a single massive cottonwood overshadowed the front yard, its shade deep and wide.

"Nice place," Bannerman observed.

"Sam Burns don't do things by the half," Kidder said.

We waited by the gate of the fence, and Bannerman reached down to rumple the ears of a large dog that seemed to have adopted him. After having both ears attended, the dog flopped down, rolling on its back, presenting a wide, white belly. The banker rubbed the offered belly with the toe of his boot.

"Good watch dog," he said.

Kidder grunted and then straightened up from his leaning against the low fence.

"Afternoon, Mr. Burns," he said and touched the brim of his hat.

I don't know what I had expected, but the Sam Burns that stood on the stoop of the house was nothing like I had pictured. He was an old man, very short, with a ruff of white hair that framed an otherwise bald head. His eyebrows were the same white, shaggy and full. He stumped down the steps and across the yard toward us, hands on hips, looking behind us first to the right and then the left.

"What do I owe this honor, Deputy?" he asked, and his voice was deep and rich with just a hint of a burr.

"Well, sir, this here is Dr. Robert Patterson. He's a doc down in Cooperville. And this here is John Bannerman, from the same. And you know me, I guess. Bernie Kidder, work for Max Edmunds."

Burns nodded, noncommittal, waiting for the deputy to get to the point. Kidder did, sketching out the details of why he had come. Burns listened tight-lipped, arms folded in front of him, not interrupting the deputy until the man was finished.

"Six head, you say?"

Kidder nodded.

Burns looked at me. "How far is it from here to Cooperville, anyway. It's been years since I was over that way."

I glanced at Bannerman. "Forty miles, would you say, John?"

"Closer to thirty," Kidder said. "Ranch here is actually closer to Cooperville than Coldwater."

"That's not out of reason, then," Burns said, musing. "Whether I lost six head or not, I couldn't confirm, Deputy. At least not right now. Not without a head count. Six out of more than a thousand is hardly noticed, unless you catch the bastards red-handed. It wouldn't be hard to take six—or sixty, for that matter." He shrugged. "Rustling is not a new pastime for some of the folks around here," he said with a hint of bitterness.

"I gather," he continued, looking at me again, "that your concern is not with the rustling but with the anthrax."

"Yes, sir. If six animals can be sick, then a whole herd might be infected."

"I'd hate to think that was true," Burns said. "To my knowledge, there's never been any of that sickness on my range."

"The six cattle got it somewhere."

"I'm not questioning your expertise, Doctor. And I'm somewhat chagrined that some of my stock should cause such anguish to so many people. Naturally, I'm at your disposal, for whatever you think should be done." He turned and gestured at the house. "Shall we go inside? I'm sure you gentlemen would appreciate being able to take your ease in something other than a saddle."

We followed him inside, into a house that was comfortable and well appointed. His wife, a full head taller than him, greeted us politely, made sure we had refreshments, although we were not offered dinner just then, and then excused herself from the room, leaving the four of us to talk.

Kidder showed Burns the poster, and the rancher

looked at the face for a long time, turning the poster this way and that. He finally handed it back to the deputy and shook his head. "Never seen the man," he said. "What's your plans?"

"I'd like to look at your herd, Mr. Burns," I said quickly.

"You think that's necessary?" Kidder asked, impatient. "Christ almighty, that could take you a month."

"Yes, I think it's necessary," I said.

Burns leaned forward. "Doctor, is there some condition, anything at all, that favors the anthrax? Is there anything we can be looking for? I have men in my employ, and they can help. But we need to know what to look for. If the cattle got sick on my land, then something must be causing it."

"Anthrax is a soil bacterium," I said. "Fortunately the instances of livestock coming in contact with it, enough to become infected, are rare. From what I've read about it, wet conditions that seasonally dry up lend themselves. An infected animal left untended in pasturage with other livestock. Any number of things."

"That doesn't make the job any easier," Burns said. "I'm no more than a month away from driving my cattle to the railhead. The last thing I'd want is to ship a herd of infected cattle. I'd never sell another beef. Not to mention the other consequences."

Kidder slapped his thigh idly. "Well, gents, you may want to look at cows, but I got me other errands."

"You going on after Brown?" Bannerman asked.

"Might as well have a look see in this neighborhood," the deputy said easily. "Thought I'd go on into Thatcher and ask around. Maybe ride on up to Colby, then over to Animas. Tell you what. I'll plan to come on by here again, let's say about three days. That ought to give the doc enough time to be sick of lookin' at cows. And I'll have covered a patch of ground. We'll figure out what to do from there." He stood up, as if that ended the conversation.

"John, what do you plan to do?" I asked.

The banker nodded reluctantly. "I'll give you a hand here."

"Then I'll be on my way," Kidder said and picked up his hat.

"How about some food before you go?" Burns said and got up as well. "I suspect you're all on the hungry side."

"Why sure," the deputy said and dropped his hat back in the chair.

Early the next morning, with Deputy Bernie Kidder already ten hours on the trail toward Thatcher and Colby, Bannerman and I shared the breakfast table with the Burnses, including their oldest son. He was short, like his father, and tight-lipped, like his mother.

And then we began an organized survey of the Burns's ranch. Seven men, including three that we met running fence south of the house, helped us, and I got the impression that the cowboys thought me somewhat daft.

Sam Burns sent his son and another cowpuncher north, toward the main herd, with instructions from me about what to look for. After the others had their instructions and an area to cover, Burns, Bannerman, and I rode south toward the river.

We passed by a herd of ten or so, and they loped off at our approach, tails lashing, clumsy and uncollected in gait.

"If they're running, there's little chance they're sick,"

I said, and we sat watching the animals slow down as they drew away to a safe distance.

In one spot the thickets along the river were nearly impenetrable. The land was flat but protected on all sides by the brush and deadfall from the cottonwoods that lined the small stream.

"Damnest spot," Burns remarked as we skirted the area. "Almost lost one of my men here six or seven years ago in the quicksand. He was chasin' a few head, and one of 'em ducked into the brush like a damned rabbit. He rode in after 'em and said later he damned near didn't make it back out."

"Your roundup must take you some time," I said.

Burns nodded. "Getting to be more work every year, for me at least. Gonna have to give it up one of these times and let the boy take it over."

"He looks ready," Bannerman remarked. "Stout lad."

"Takes after his mother," Burns said. "We don't run many head down this way," he continued. "There's better places to water up north and easier to run the cattle, too. There's always some down here, though. Always some that has to do life the hard way."

We rounded the end of the thicket and stopped. Two steers stood by the brush, staring at us. Neither one shifted a foot but instead stood, as if rooted. They watched us as we spurred the horses closer, but they showed no sign of moving away.

"There's one down in the brush," Bannerman said, his sharp eyes catching the outline of another steer.

"Just resting," Burns said, but his voice was uneasy.

He rode over and then sharply reined the horse to a standstill. "Dead," he said flatly. I dropped the reins from Clara's neck and slid down, holding her short so she couldn't graze.

"Keep your mount out of the grass," I said to the others, and they sat watching me. I handed Clara's reins to Bannerman and made my way cautiously toward the two steers. One didn't even bother to turn its head, but the other did, regarding me with eyes that were red-rimmed. I walked around the animals, noticing that they had no control of their bowels. And then I could see the carbuncles, rough, ugly lumps in the smooth hide of their necks and underneath on their bellies.

"They're sick," I called and heard Sam Burns curse. I walked back to where they held the horses. "Those cattle will have to be put down."

Face grim, Burns pulled his rifle from the saddle scabbard and spurred his horse forward. His mount flinched as the heavy rifle boomed so close to his ear, and first one steer and then the other pitched down into the soft dirt. Burns had never questioned my judgment.

I turned and surveyed the thicket around which we had just ridden, seeing it in a new light.

"I'll lay a bet the anthrax got started in there," I said. "Sick cattle don't move far. Not willingly. I say we cover that brush from one end to the other."

Burns cradled the rifle across his thighs. "You aren't going to be able to ride a horse through there," he observed.

"Nor would I want to," I said and thought uneasily about even walking through. As far as I knew, the cattle had contracted the bacilli by grazing grass right down to the nubs. There was little danger, if any, of walking there, but it was just the idea of it all. The anthrax seemed almost like an evil thing, waiting. "You say you don't get down here much, nor do your men. It's not surprising to me that you wouldn't have seen any signs of sickness." I swung down from Clara, knowing that in all likelihood we had found the source of the contagion. If the cattle wandered into the thicket and grazed, it was entirely possible that they would take sick before the notion ever entered their thick, slow-witted skulls to move back up range.

"John, why don't you stay here and hold the horses. Try to keep them from grazing," I said.

He nodded. "I'll ride back upstream, to the other end of the thicket," he said. "Meet you there." I took my rifle and joined Burns, and we plunged into the thick tangle. We found only one other steer, listless and in the last stages of the fast-acting disease. Burns shot it, and I bent over, examining it without touching the hide.

"There's no doubt," I said at length, straightening up. We pressed on, finding nothing more than the remains of another steer, long dead, nothing left but picked-over bones. "That animal may have been the first," I said.

Burns stopped, scratching his head. "I don't figure," he said, "that I understand any of this. How in hell can animals get so sick that they won't even move, and still a rustler can take six of them and drive them thirty miles. That just don't make no sense to me. Does it to you?"

"Once an animal gets the contagion, then it's got about two, maybe at the most four days. I'd think a cow is like anything else that gets sick. They start to feel poorly and just kind of lose the determination to move."

"That still doesn't explain them sick here and ending up thirty miles away in Cooperville."

I stopped and looked around us, trying to peer through the brush. "The only answer I can think of is that whoever took the cattle passed through here on their way out of your territory."

"You mean they camped here, while they took my cattle?"

"They might have. Look at it this way. There were three men. Your stock is scattered. They camp somewhere around here, as hidden as if they had found themselves a hole in the ground. I don't know anything about cattle, or rustling, but it would seem to me that one man could just as easily keep the cattle rounded up in some spot that was protected from view in any direction, while the other two bring more in."

"Then they might have taken more than six."

"Maybe. But we'll never know until we have a chance to chat with Mr. Brown."

"Brown?"

"Blaine, then. The face on the poster."

Burns swore again. "He's a fella I'd like to talk to, but with this," and he lifted the rifle slightly.

We moved on, and just before the river cut us off, forcing us to turn slightly eastward to follow the thicket, we saw the remains of the campfire.

Burns glanced at me, one eyebrow uplifted.

"Would one of your men camp here?"

He shook his head. "We got line shacks every so often that they use." He grinned humorlessly. "They're used to their comforts."

"Hunters, maybe."

"Not likely, out here. Trappers either. I'm guessing that you're right. The rustlers camped here, at least one night." He frowned. "Not too good at their job, it seems to me."

"Why?"

"Most rustlers I've ever known never stayed lit in one spot long enough to have a camp. I sure as hell wouldn't if I had a handful of my neighbor's cattle."

"Blaine's a killer, for low stakes, at that," I said. "I'm not convinced that rustling is his game. He tried it once, made a few dollars. Lost two partners. From what Sheriff Edmunds said down in Coldwater, he's a man that works alone, most of the time."

"Likes to try his hand at a number of things," Burns said, and he spat on the ground at his feet. We continued on, finding nothing more. Still, I was convinced and told Bannerman so when we emerged at the north end of the thicket.

"Let's assume that this is the only spot where there's a problem, Doc," Burns said, shoving his rifle back in the saddle scabbard. "What you figure I ought to do?"

"Well, you can't just burn the thicket. That wouldn't touch any of the contagion that's in the soil now. The grass would just grow back, and things might be worse than they are now." I turned, looking behind me at the rise of the land over which we had ridden. "If I was you, I'd run a strong wire fence, cutting off this entire part of your range. Maybe start a thousand yards or more back up the hill and continue it all the way down south, to where the land rises again." I pointed south and then across the river. "And I'd fence off the other bank of the river too, right down across the water, cutting off this section of creek. Make it tight so no more cattle, horses, men, or anything else is bound to get into that thicket. You're lucky it tends to lie in a low spot."

"That's a lot of fence," Burns observed. He looked wryly at John Bannerman. "Your bank good for a loan, you think?"

There was no way a man like Burns needed a loan of a few dollars for some rolled wire, not with a spread the size of his, and Bannerman just laughed politely at the weak joke.

"All right," Burns said and shifted in his saddle. "I'm glad we found it, and thanks to you gentlemen for your efforts. I'm not sure I would have gone to such bother if I were in your boots." We hadn't told him the specifics of who had died in Cooperville. I avoided mentioning it for Bannerman's sake. Sam Burns had no way of realizing that our trip was more than just a case of civic bother.

CHAPTER 11

With our business finished so quickly at the Burns ranch, John Bannerman and I elected to ride on to Thatcher, and even to Colby, catching up with Deputy Bernie Kidder. Sam Burns had made it clear that we were welcome to spend the time at his ranch, waiting for the deputy's return, but I could see that Bannerman was impatient to be moving. Sitting still just seemed to make matters worse for him.

It was less than a day's ride to Thatcher, only twelve miles, and on a fairly good trail, cut deep from the passage of wagons. We had spent only a morning with Burns, examining the cattle, and we left his ranch in the early afternoon, hoping to catch up with the slow-moving Kidder before he got all the way to Colby. Burns had assured us that the only route back from Colby was through Thatcher, and then the road back to the ranch, and we felt it unlikely that we would miss Kidder if he was heading back already.

We rode steadily, keeping the horses in a trot or an easy lope when the ground suited, and reached Thatcher by midafternoon. Kidder had been there, we were told, but hadn't tarried long. Colby was another eighteen miles, a larger town than Thatcher, nestled in the foothills, a mining town with lumbering going on in the hills as well.

We watered the horses and ourselves, and Bannerman

insisted we ride on. My bottom was already sore, but I agreed. Thatcher was nothing more than a crossroad, and there was nothing there for us except the brief refreshment. We pushed the horses a little faster than I would have liked, and during the three-hour ride to Colby, my companion didn't say more than a half-dozen words—most of them curses when a wasp sang by and stung him in the neck.

"Ever notice those creatures fly tail first?" I said, hoping the humor would stir some life into my partner. But Bannerman just grunted and cussed again, rubbing his neck. He spurred his horse a little faster, and I gave up my attempts to carry on a conversation with him.

We reached Colby at exactly six o'clock. It was a thriving town, with two hotels and more saloons than I cared to count. Up on the hillsides I could see several mines dotting the landscape, and to the north, a chip burner belched dark smoke above a small, neat lumberyard.

It was not difficult finding Bernie Kidder. He was standing on the boardwalk talking with another man, and he saw us ride in.

"My escort," he said to the man and stepped forward as we dismounted. "Get your fill of looking at cows?"

"That's all settled," I said, pushing my hat back on my head. I stretched and shook my head. "We figured we might as well tail you here and see what you found."

Kidder grinned. "Well, we had us some luck, I guess."

"You found out something about Blaine?" Bannerman asked quickly.

"Yup," Kidder said. "Spent part of the afternoon tryin' to talk to him. Like talkin' to a rattlesnake."

"You mean he's here?"

"Yup."

"Well, where the hell is he?" Bannerman said, a tremor in his voice.

Kidder jerked a thumb up the street. "Jail's up that way. He's coolin' his heels." He turned and looked at the other man. "This here's town marshal of Colby. Ray Johnson. Ray, this is the doc and the banker I was tellin' you about." Kidder was his usual self, not in a hurry.

"How'd you catch Blaine?" I asked, still incredulous that our search had ended so effortlessly.

Johnson looked kind of proud of himself. "He was playin' cards over at the Trail's End, over there. Things got kind of out of hand, and he pulled a gun on the gent that was dealin'. Or at least tried to. One of the other boys beat him to it. They said he was cheatin' and would have shot each other to pieces right then and there. I happened to be passin' by and ducked in to see what the row was all about."

"He just let you take him?" I asked.

"Well, now, he didn't much have a choice. I got me this shotgun," and he swung the old scatter-gun up, "and he seemed to see the error of his ways. Said he'd had too much to drink, so I allowed as to how I had just the right place for him to sleep it off."

"So you locked him up."

"Yes sir, I did that. Not that that jail's much good, but it'll serve. Weren't no more than an hour later that the deputy here rode into town, and as a matter of course, he said what his business was all about. I took one look at that there poster of his and about dropped my drawers. Didn't know what sort of fish I'd landed." He laughed as if the whole thing was a great joke. "If the deputy hadn't showed, why I would have just let him go once he was sobered up."

"I wonder why he came here," I said, mystified, but Bannerman was in no mood to talk idly on the boardwalk.

"I want to see him," he said.

"That can be arranged," the marshal said, still proud of himself. "Yes sir, that can be arranged. Can't it, Deputy?"

"Yes," Kidder said, but his face was serious. "Mr. Bannerman, you can see him, but you give me your six-gun when you go in there."

The banker looked at the young lawman for a full minute, and I wondered what was going through his mind.

"All right," he said at last. "You can have the gun." He pulled out the Colt and handed it butt first to Kidder, who took it and thrust it into his own belt.

"You carrying?" Kidder said to me.

"Just the rifle," I said. I held out my coat to show him that I didn't have a revolver hidden away.

"All right. It would be best to get you to identify him anyway, just to make double sure. He ain't so much as told me his name, and I ain't told him why he's wanted. He might just be a little nasty when he finds out for sure his trail's ended."

We walked up the hot, dusty street, and I repeated an early question to Kidder. "Why did he come here, you figure?"

The deputy shrugged. "Creatures of habit don't generally cover all that much ground," he said. "This is a bit far from his stompin' grounds, but it's a right rich little town. Lots of opportunity here." He shrugged. "Hell, he's got to be somewhere, ain't he? Might as well be here. We was bound to catch up with him sooner or later."

The jail was indeed a crude affair, but it was stoutly constructed, a stone addition to the marshal's office and home, with a heavy iron-barred door giving access directly from the marshal's office. The two windows in the cell were nothing more than slits in the stone, with no bars, the openings so small a rat would have had difficulty entering. I noticed that there was no provision for heat, other than what drifted in from the marshal's office, and nothing other than a bucket for sanitation. Then I stopped noticing the furnishings, because I saw Aloysius Blaine sitting on the floor in the dark corner.

He saw the deputy first, and his expression didn't change from one of flat contempt. Then he saw me, and his face drained color. He turned his head quickly toward the wall, as if to prevent me from recognizing him, but it did no good. I would never have forgotten that face.

"That the man?" Kidder asked.

I nodded. "That's the man."

"Then we got our man," the deputy said. "We'll start for Coldwater in the morning," he said to the marshal. "You'd best dig out a pair of leg irons, if you got 'em. We're going to take real good care of this bird."

I looked at Bannerman, but he was just standing quietly by the door of the cell, eyes fixed on the man inside. Blaine had not spoken a word and had not turned around, but it was almost as if there was some kind of tangible communication between the two men. The outlaw turned slowly, and his eyes met Bannerman's. The two men stared at each other, Blaine's expression mildly curious but otherwise devoid of emotion. It was the first time I had ever seen such hatred on John Bannerman's face.

Without breaking his gaze, the banker said quietly, "So this is the man who killed my wife."

He said nothing else, and up to then Blaine had had no way of making the connection. He had had no way of knowing, short of being told outright, about the havoc the sick cattle had wrought after he sold them. Kidder hadn't told him, apparently, but must have played cat and mouse with him all afternoon, seeing what he could get the man to admit. Blaine, at that moment, was probably thinking about the killing down in Bayard—the woman and the nineteen dollars.

Whatever he was thinking, it was Marshal Johnson who provided the outlaw with the full story.

"You wonder what kind of a man would do something like that," he said, walking away from the doorway to the cell where we had been standing. "Rustle a handful of sick cattle, then sell 'em without givin' a thought to who might get sick." He shook his head, but I didn't reply. I saw the light of understanding come into those dead eyes of Blaine's. He shifted his stare from Bannerman's face to mine. I saw there a kind of sorrow, but a sorrow that chilled me to the bone. I could read Blaine's thoughts as if they were printed on the wall. He had ridden away from the camp, his two sick companions, and me, knowing that the two companions would die and not caring about me. Now he cared. The look in his eyes was one of pure malice, pure hate for the one man who had been responsible for his coming to terms with the law.

Both John Bannerman and I spent a restless night—at least the first few hours of it. We checked into one of the hotels, had a hot meal, and retired to our room. Bannerman looked worn out, looking his age and then some. The thirst for revenge, or for justice, that had driven him on the trail was gone now, and he seemed anxious to return to Cooperville, to try to take up where he had left off. We talked for a while and then went to bed, thinking we were tired enough to sleep. We both were exhausted, but sleep would not come. We lay on our backs, staring at the ceiling of the musty hotel room, listening to the sounds of the village outside and below us.

"You think Kidder will have any trouble getting Blaine down to Coldwater?" Bannerman finally said. I stirred and shifted position in the short bed.

"I shouldn't think so. He knows his job. You heard him ask about leg irons."

"How in hell do you ride a horse with leg irons on?" Bannerman asked.

"I don't know. I suppose the chain is long enough that it loops up over the saddle. I've never tried it."

Bannerman grunted. "I'm not sure I'd want to either."

After a moment, I said, "What do you think the courts will do with Blaine?"

"Hang the son of a bitch," Bannerman replied with considerable venom. "He murdered that woman and then at least four others by proxy. Maybe they'll hang him for that shooting in Denver Edmunds was talking about."

"I always wonder what drives a person like that."

"He's just a mad animal. Like a dog with rabies. No sense of right or wrong."

"You figure Kidder is sleeping over at the jail tonight?"

For the first time Bannerman chuckled. "No, I don't figure that. There's a young man with a great deal of self-confidence. He'll sleep like a baby tonight and get up first light tomorrow fresh as a daisy. I imagine he found himself the best room in the best hotel in this town."

"There's only two hotels in this town."

"Then he's in the best one. Which isn't this one, incidentally."

"We didn't have to come here."

"It was closest. Hell of a thing."

"What?"

"A bank president and a physician sleeping in a place like this."

"It's not that bad, John."

"Your knees aren't hanging over the end of the mattress."

"It's better than a bedroll out on a limestone outcrop," I said, remembering the ride north to Burns's ranch.

"That I'll agree with."

The hours dragged by, and once or twice I awoke with a start, surprised that I had been asleep in the first place. Once I thought I heard voices down in the street, but I paid no attention. Bannerman seemed to be asleep, his breathing now regular and slow. I must have dozed off again, because I remember one thing with absolute certainty—the gunshot woke me.

CHAPTER 12

The shot was single, echoing up and down the quiet predawn street of Colby. I had been sleeping so lightly that it jarred me upright, and it was more the motion of me in the soft bed, rather than the shot, that brought John Bannerman half out of his deep, almost drugged sleep.

"Huh?" he muttered, then saw me sitting up.

"Sh," I whispered, for I was waiting for another shot, something to fix direction. There was nothing for several seconds, and I began to relax. "I think it was a gunshot," I said.

"Gunshot?" Bannerman grunted and rubbed his face. "The drunks at it again?"

I turned and slipped out of bed, making my way barefoot to the window. We were on the second floor, and the window faced the main street of Colby. At first I saw no one, then I recognized a figure, racing right down the middle of the street. It was Bernie Kidder, hatless, bootless, in his underwear and trousers. I saw the glint of a revolver in his hands, and then he ducked up onto the boardwalk, and I lost him under the overhanging eaves. He was running toward the marshal's office and jail.

"John, I think there's trouble," I said and started pulling on my pants and shirt. I had them almost on when a second shot rang out, and I heard a single cry of pain. There were shouts, and I took a moment to look out the window again. Two or three others were in the street now, and then two shots crashed down the street. I saw a horse kicked sideways away from the hitching post down street, and then there was a man mounted, thrashing the horse for all he was worth. Another shot peeled out, and I saw the horse take a funny, crabbing step sideways, then continue pell-mell down the street, the rider bent low over its neck.

And then the lights came on. It seemed like every lantern along the main street of Colby blossomed with light, the triangles and squares and cones of illumination spreading out into the dirt of the thoroughfare.

I was dressed and out the door, then flung back into the room on second thought, grabbing my medical bag. Bannerman was out of bed, pulling on his clothes. "I'll meet you down there," I said and raced out.

"Be careful," I heard him call after me, and then I was beyond hearing, taking the stairs two and three and four at a time, bursting out through the small lobby and into the cool of the night. The moon was almost harshly bright, and I raced down the street toward the marshal's office, nearing the group of people who crowded the walkway. There were so many, in various stages of wakefulness or alertness, that I wondered what percentage of Colby's population never went to bed at night.

"Over here," someone shouted at me. They must have seen my medical bag, and it was medicine that was needed then. I skidded to a halt beside a prone shape, with two men standing close by. "There's others inside," the same voice said.

"One thing at a time," I snapped and quickly examined the man. "This one is beyond anything I can do," I said and stood up abruptly. He had been taken smack in the middle of the forehead by a bullet and no doubt had been dead before his face hit the dust. There was a nearly solid wall of people between me and the jail area, and I pushed my way through roughly. "Let me through," I yelled. "I'm a physician!" The wall parted, mostly curious faces looking at me, maybe wondering who I was.

I pushed my way inside the office and nearly tripped over another body. "Someone get some light in here," I shouted, and several obliged, bringing two kerosene lanterns over in short order.

The man I had nearly fallen over was deputy Bernie Kidder. I knelt down and gently turned him over and was rewarded with a stifled groan.

"Bernie," I said. "You can hear me?"

"Christ, yes, I hear you. Stop shoutin'."

I realized I had been and helped the deputy into a sitting position against the wall.

"What happened?"

Kidder clenched his teeth and slowly pounded the floor with his left hand in a mixture of rage, pain, and frustration.

"That son of a bitch broke jail," he said and looked at me, eyes barely open.

He had taken a shotgun blast in the right side, the pattern small and at close range. The charge had nicked the inside of his right arm, tearing the muscle badly, but the main force of the heavy pellets had laced across his ribs, and I could see a chip of bone that I took to be part of a rib showing wetly through what was left of his long johns.

I started to pull the clothing away, but he reached up and touched me with his left hand. I looked at his face, and he nodded across the room. "Take a look at the marshal," he said weakly. "I'll be all right."

"You'll bleed to death if you don't shut up and let me work," I said and pushed his hand away.

"Damn it, Doc, look at the marshal. I got to know what happened, and he knows. Now I'll be all right."

"Marshal's hurt bad," someone said in my ear, and I glanced up into a sea of concerned faces.

"Why don't some of you people clear out of here so a man can work," I snapped, and a couple of them backed away. I saw John Bannerman, his big frame filling the doorway.

"John, clear these people out of here," I shouted and out of the corner of my eye saw Kidder wince again and shake his head. "I mean it. John, get these people the hell out of here."

Bannerman moved fast, hustling folks away, turning the curious in the opposite direction. A couple resisted, and Bannerman didn't stop for negotiations. He simply took them by the collar and shoved them out the door, until just the two of us and the wounded were left in the room.

In the meantime I got up and stepped over to Marshal Johnson. He was hurt, mortally so. The shotgun charge had hit him squarely in the gut, and he was lying in a puddle of blood that spread out on the board floor.

"Blaine," he said, voice almost inaudible.

Almost without looking, I prepared a syringe and a heavy dose of morphine, stabbing it into his arm and pushing the big plunger home. There was little else I could do.

"What happened?" I said, leaning close so I could hear. The marshal's eyes didn't focus for a moment, then he seemed to latch onto my face, and one hand came up from the floor to catch hold of my shirt sleeve.

"He called for the doc," the marshal whispered. "Said he was havin' con . . . con . . ."

"Convulsions?"

Johnson nodded feebly.

"Said he had the anthra . . . anthrax."

"Anthrax?"

"Said he needed a doc. I didn't . . . didn't know where you was, so I got Doc Davis."

I looked up and caught Bannerman's eye. "John, check in the cell."

"He killed him," the marshal said, whimpering. "Took him by the neck and made me give him the shotgun. Then he just broke his neck, like a . . . like a dog." He lapsed into agonizing silence, lips pressed tight together. "Ain't there nothing that you can do for me, Doc?" he managed finally.

"I just gave you an injection. It should help soon," I said, feeling helpless.

"There's an old man in there, dead," I heard Bannerman say. Then another voice, outside, yelled at us.

"Let us in there!" he said.

Bannerman strode to the door and opened it with a yank and closed it behind him. After that, no one else asked to come inside.

"Blaine killed the doctor?" I asked, and Johnson didn't answer at once but finally moved his lips some, and then I had to lean closer still to hear him.

"Killed him, then just up and shot me, without givin' me a chance. Then . . . then he just stood there and waited, smilin'." The marshal opened his eyes wide and raised his head. "Smilin'! Like it was some big joke. He just stood there, smilin', and waited 'till Bernie run up. Then he shot him too."

He struggled, almost as if he wanted to sit up, then flopped back on the floor, flat on his back. His eyes were staring at the ceiling, and then they glazed and he stopped breathing.

"Christ Almighty," I muttered and stood up. I looked at the marshal for a moment, then walked to the cell. The man there was ancient, well past seventy, and now nothing more than a thin bundle of clothing. I checked for a pulse and found none.

"You bastard," I said aloud. I wondered what the outcome would have been if the marshal had fetched me instead of the old physician, the man he had probably known for years.

"Doc . . ."

I turned and hurried back over to Bernie Kidder.

"I'm feelin' awful cold, Doc."

"Shock," I said, not liking the pallor of the young deputy's face. "We got to get you to some help."

"You're help," and he grinned weakly.

"Not here. I need more than just this black bag." I remembered with frustration that I had packed my bag with anthrax in mind, not gunshots. I swiftly opened the door, seeing nothing but Bannerman's broad back when I did so. He turned and raised an eyebrow.

"John, we've got to get the deputy to an infirmary, or something. Even the old doc's office would do."

Bannerman turned and gestured at one of the men who stood in a silent ring around the walk in front of the marshal's office. And in short order they lifted Kidder gently to his feet and half carried, half walked him out into the night. The office of Gordon Davis was a full three blocks from where the shooting had taken place, and before they were halfway there, they had lifted the deputy clear of the ground, carrying him along swiftly, almost at a trot. Bannerman followed along, and before we went inside, he touched my arm.

"Robert."

"Yes?" I turned, impatient to be inside and working.

"I'm going after him."

I looked at the big banker for a moment, not believing what I had just heard.

"You're what?"

"I said I'm going after him."

"You're out of your mind."

"Maybe that's true. But that's what I'm going to do."

"John, for God's sake, he kills without so much as a blink! Did you see what he did?" I waved back down the street.

"I saw."

"Well, use some common sense. Leave it for the law."

"And someone else will get killed," Bannerman said harshly.

"Yes. You, most likely. You're not a young man any longer. Remember that."

Bannerman ignored that, looking down the street. "He rode up toward the mines, up there on the hill. Someone said his horse was hit by gunfire. At least two men shot at him as he rode away. I've got a good chance."

"No chance," I said, angry.

Bannerman turned and looked at me, face tense.

"The longer I wait, the farther he'll get."

"I've got work to do," I said sharply. "Don't be a fool. I may need your help."

Bannerman shook his head. "There's nothing I can help you with, Robert. You're the doctor. I'll not keep you." And with that, he turned on his heel and strode off into the darkness.

"Goddamned stubborn people," I cursed and entered the office of Gordon Davis, murdered doctor of Colby. Maybe Bannerman would organize a posse, I thought, but as quickly dismissed the idea. It wasn't his way.

As soon as I had Kidder's wound cleaned free of clothing, bits of wadding, and pellets, I saw why Blaine had been able to ride away. Even if he had had the strength, the musculature of his right arm was so damaged Bernie Kidder would not have been able to fire a shot. No doubt Blaine thought he had killed the deputy, but from the path of the pellets I guessed that Kidder had twisted at the last moment. Instead of ripping straight into the right side of his chest, the charge had passed between arm and body, doing damage to both but not creating a fatal wound.

The old doctor had a well-appointed office, the product of a long and fruitful practice cut short senselessly by a man not worth a tenth of Davis's life. I helped Kidder up onto the smooth operating table, and he gritted his teeth.

"Damn," he said and then grinned up at me. "This is the first time," he said.

"For what?"

"Catchin' lead like this."

"May it be the last, Deputy."

"You going to give me a bullet to bite?"

"Hell no. I'm going to give you ether so you'll sleep like a babe and be out of my hair."

Kidder glanced down at his arm, now bare, and then at the side of his torso, ragged and torn. "I guess that would be best," he said and relaxed back on the table.

I worked for more than an hour and after the first fifteen minutes had the help of an earnest old woman who said she had been Dr. Davis's nurse. She had tears in her eyes the whole time, and I was too busy to offer her much comfort. But she was an efficient and well-trained assistant. At one point she was a little slow in getting a suture length out of the phenol, and I snapped my fingers impatiently.

"Come on, come on," I said.

The suture and needle slapped into my hand with somewhat more force than I thought necessary, and I glanced at her, irritated. The tears were flowing down her cheeks, unchecked, and she was shaking with silent sobs.

"Ma'am, I'm truthfully sorry about what happened," I said. "I'm sure Dr. Davis was a fine physician. What happened was senseless. I wish . . ." and I stopped talking while I tied a difficult knot, "I wish there was something I could do to make it easier for you."

She sniffled and dabbed at her nose.

"How long did the doctor practice here in Colby?"

"Ten years."

"And you worked with him all that time?"

"Yes."

"That must have been an experience," I said, hoping the conversation would jar her out of her sorrow. She was making the surgery difficult then. I was trying to close the wound in the arm with great care, repairing the torn muscle, hoping that the deputy would regain the use of the member.

Instead of telling me what an experience it had been, the woman sobbed and drew away from the table.

I shook my head. "When you feel better, I need some bandaging," I said gently. "Use iodine, not carbolic acid. I don't want any more irritation than necessary." She nodded, her back to me and the table, and moved away to do as I asked.

When I had finished, I turned to the woman, who was making an effort to clean up the mess around the table. "Why don't you leave that," I said, taking her by the arm. "I'll get it. You best be home in bed." She clung to my arm for a moment, and I saw she wasn't as elderly as I had first assumed. Life in Colby hadn't been easy on her, evidently.

"I thank you for helping," I said, looking for something else to say, and she raised a tear-stained face, blinking back the stream of droplets that kept creeping from the corners of her eyes.

"He was such a good man," she said and pulled out a hanky from the depths of her long dress, mopping her nose and then dabbing at her eyes. "I'm sorry I wasn't able to control myself. I shall miss him so."

"I'm sure we all will," I said soothingly.

"He was my brother," she said simply and dabbed at her eyes again.

"Good God," I breathed, feeling like a swine. I put my arm around her shoulders and could feel the shaking again. She was on the brink of collapse, having used up all her energy in one herculean effort of will to come to her brother's office to assist me, even while the old man lay dead in a jail cell down the street. "I'd best see you home," I said.

Bernie Kidder came out of the ether quickly, and as soon as he was fully conscious and aware of his surroundings, he flashed his characteristic grin, though now somewhat feeble and halfhearted.

"I'm a mess," he said softly, trying to lift his head.

"Lie quiet. It's going to be several days before you feel like moving an inch."

I looked around the office, knowing I couldn't move Kidder without causing him unbearable pain. There was a divan of sorts in the next room, nowhere long enough but considerably softer than the table on which the deputy lay. I skidded the divan through the doorway and into the room where Kidder watched. I slid the divan right up to the table and motioned. "We're going to put you on that," I said. "It will be more comfortable."

"All right." It was easier said than done, but with grunts from me and gasps from Kidder, the job got done, with him lying on his back, white-faced and exhausted.

His eyes opened and he asked, "What became of Blaine?"

"He got away."

"After all that shootin'?"

"Folks around here don't practice on rabbits on the fly," I said wryly.

"I walked right into it, didn't I?"

"Yes, you did."

"He meant to kill me."

"Yes."

"I wished you could have seen his face."

"I'm just as glad I missed it."

"That fella's loco, Doc. Just out of his mind."

"Yes."

"They form a posse?"

"I don't think so."

"Damn gutless wonders."

"They're not lawmen, Bernie. That was Johnson's job. He's dead. I'd guess they want to wait and see what you want to do."

"Ain't much I can do now."

"John Bannerman rode out after him." I felt sick saying that, thinking about that.

"The big banker? Damn, he's an old man!"

"Say that to his face, Bernie. He's no older than Max Edmunds."

Kidder grinned and turned his head so he was looking up the back of the divan, maybe trying to lose his pain in the intricate pattern of the coverlet that lay over the back. "Edmunds is an old man too. But a good one." He turned and looked at me again.

"Blaine will kill your friend."

I finished cleaning up and turned to glare at Kidder. "You don't need to tell me that."

"He shoulda waited."

"Of course he should have, Deputy. But that man killed his wife, for Christ's sake. We thought he was in custody, and then he killed three more men, almost four, if your lucky stars hadn't been shining. He came along with us to see Blaine put away." I shrugged and sat down in a straight-backed chair. "Now I guess he's going to try to do that on his own."

"What you aim to do?"

I sat quietly for a moment, knowing what I would do but not wanting to admit to myself yet what lay before me.

"You're goin' after 'em, ain't you?"

Kidder was looking at me, appraising, no grin on his face then.

"I guess I am."

"You got a gun?"

"Rifle."

Kidder nodded. "My gun's over there, where you stripped it off me. Belt ought to fit you all right. Take it along."

I picked up the gun belt, hefting its dead weight in my hand.

"You oughta get somebody to go with you, you know."

"I'm no hero."

Kidder grinned. "You're going to have troubles, pal. I heard them talkin' outside the office, callin' Blaine a mad dog. Folks don't much like chasin' mad dogs. That's why they hire fellas like me."

"You're encouraging."

Kidder twisted position slightly and sucked air between his teeth.

"You all right?"

"Dandy," he said. "Ain't you got any pain killer?"

"Morphine, if you want it."

"I was thinkin' of somethin' that tasted kind of good while I was drinkin' it."

"I'll see what I can find. Probably do you a world of good."

I rummaged around the old doctor's office and found nothing more than a third-full bottle of peach brandy. I took the cork out and handed the bottle to Kidder, who inspected the label critically. He looked askance at me, then sampled the brandy, making a face.

"This don't taste good," he said flatly.

"The best I can do. Look, if you think you'll be all right, I need to go."

Kidder held up the bottle and nodded. I turned to leave, and he said, "Doc."

"What?"

"Take my badge."

"What for?"

"So when you shoot the bastard, you do it legal."

"I hadn't planned on shooting him. I intend to bring him back for justice."

Kidder laughed, and then coughed, and then let out a little cry of pain. "Damn." He looked at me. "You're more of a fool than I thought, then," he said finally, catching his breath. "Blaine ain't going to let you bring him back nowheres. You see him, you shoot him. Don't be a goddamn fool, Doc." He set the bottle on the floor near him. "Now get the badge off my shirt."

I didn't wish to argue with the deputy, so I unpinned the heavy metal badge and started to hand it to him. He shook his head. "I don't want it. You pin it on."

I looked at the star, frowning.

"Raise your right hand."

"What?"

"You know your right from your left? Then raise it."

"Don't be ridiculous. This isn't even legal."

"The hell you say. Who's going to ask? Your hand's raised. Good." It wasn't, but Kidder didn't seem to care much one way or the other. "You swear to uphold the laws of this territory and . . . the hell with it. Just pin it on, Deputy."

"Take care of yourself until I get back, Bernie," I said and turned to go, the star in my pocket, my medical bag in one hand, and the gun belt in the other.

"It's me that should be sayin' that to you, Doctor," Bernie Kidder said and grinned weakly. "You bring Blaine back, I promise you Sheriff Edmunds will let you keep that star."

"That's one promise you won't ever have to worry about keeping, Bernie." I left the office, well aware that I was getting into the habit of bringing people back from the brink of death, only to walk out on their convalescence. Tom Smith, now Bernie Kidder. I hoped they would both be alive when other duties were finished. And then another thought cropped up in my mind, so ludicrous that it kept me thinking all the way to the blacksmith-livery where my horse waited.

Which oath of office did a doctor-deputy follow? I was trained as a healer, not a lawman, but just then I didn't believe I would have any trouble making a choice when I faced Blaine, if I ever caught up with him. Maybe John Bannerman would have finished the job. And thinking about my friend, I quickened my step.

CHAPTER 13

Deputy Bernie Kidder had been entirely correct. I was alone in my desire to go up in the hills after Aloysius Blaine. The handful of men that would even talk to me were unanimous in their thinking that I was daft and that John Bannerman had been daft.

They helpfully pointed out that Blaine had been seen riding toward the hills that lay rumpled and green behind Colby, where the mine shafts dotted the slope, and beyond, where the tall pines crested the top of the ridges. Everyone agreed that the outlaw's horse had taken a bullet during his wild flight from Colby, and that was the first encouraging news I had heard. The way the horse had been smacked to one side, breaking stride, the bullet must have hit him hard. He wouldn't go far, or fast.

I saddled Clara rapidly, feeling awkward with the revolver riding against my hip but reassured by its presence. I tied my black medical bag tightly to the back of the saddle and then headed the eager horse north, toward the hills outside Colby.

I rode directly toward a cut in the trees, a hundred yards to the east of a mine shaft, the slag gray against the hillside. The people below me in the village had said they were able to watch Blaine make for that cut in the timber. They were sure, even though it had been dark. What a time to have to trust to moonlight, I thought.

They had said Bannerman had followed that route, riding hell-bent up the hill, scattering pebbles flying out from his buckskin's hooves.

With no idea of what lay ahead of me, no idea how far Bannerman had gotten in pursuit of the outlaw, I rode carefully, keeping my eyes fixed on the timber before me, half expecting to hear a shot ring out. But the hills, bathed in the morning light, were silent, ominously so. As I neared the timber, I saw a splash of blood drying on the rocky soil, and I stopped Clara. The stain wasn't large, but farther on, there were more. I booted my horse onward.

Perhaps it was entering the timber, perhaps it was simply good sense catching up with me. Whatever it was, I realized, with growing anger directed at myself, that I was a twenty-nine-year-old physician, with a long and valuable career ahead of me, tracking a friend and in front of him a killer. I had left Colby without eating breakfast, had left with no provisions of any kind—no food, water, bedroll. All I carried was two guns—a rifle and a revolver, the one almost familiar and the other strange on my hip—and a black medical bag. Those, and only the clothing on my back, and a determination that no matter how futile my chase was, it was the only thing left for me to do.

The timber was deep and thick, and I found it impossible to follow any kind of a trail. What was I supposed to be looking for? Broken twigs along the way? Blood smears on the thick pine needles under my horse's hooves? By bending low, leaning at an uncomfortable angle away from the saddle, down along Clara's neck, I was able to see vague scuff marks in the duff of the forest. There were deer trails that crisscrossed the woods, and soon I knew that it would be only luck that kept me on the trail. I thought bitterly that this was the kind of tracking a trained scout or hunter would be able to do in his sleep. I was neither.

The timber thinned at the top of the ridge, opening into a meadow that stretched out and down, the trees running along the edge to the next peak. I squinted into the early morning light, the sun just far enough above the tree line to make it difficult to see detail across the meadow and into the timber beyond. The range of hills was choppy, twisting and turning, and with no obvious trail to follow I sat on Clara, looking this way and that, wondering what to do. If a man was running, where would he go? Would he risk being seen, riding straight across the meadow for time, or would he stick to the timber, staying out of sight? I scanned the ground, looking for tracks. There were no signs I could read. Forced to make a decision of some kind, any kind, I rode boldly out across the meadow, leaving the darkness of the timber, feeling the morning sun warm on my face. If I had made no mistakes, the trail through the timber led this way. But, I thought uncomfortably, feeling like a rank amateur, I may have been following nothing more than a well-beaten and scuffed deer trail, out into a meadow where there was nothing more lethal than lupines and yarrow and grama grass.

Past the meadow, I followed the tree line around the brow of the next ridge, letting Clara step carefully where the ground narrowed past a jutting rock outcrop. We were safely around that when the shots pealed out, distant and thudding, far ahead of me and to the north. One report, then silence, then three more, quickly, then silence again, then two more shots spaced a second or two apart. I held my breath, waiting, and heard nothing more. With a curse at not knowing what the shots meant but fearing them all the more because of that, I kicked Clara savagely, and she bolted through the timber. We plunged down a slope with me trying to guide the excited horse in the general direction of the shots and yet stay in the saddle at the same time.

I ducked one limb as it whipped by, then caught another smartly in the face, making my eyes water. Barely able to see, I yanked the reins to one side as I saw Clara planning to slip by a large Douglas fir without leaving room for my leg, and I was only partly successful in changing her mind. The rough bark and spur projections of dead limbs tore at my leg, and I swore aloud. That crashing, swearing progress continued until we were off one slope and beginning to climb another. My horse shot up through the trees in a series of jackrabbit bounds, her neck pumping so far that I thought her nose would dig into the duff with each lunge. We snaked and twisted through brush and between timber until my back ached with the effort at ducking the saddle-clearing limbs that came my way. At the top of the hill, I reined in, Clara blowing hard and eyes nearly starting out of her head with excitement. She had been transformed from a sedate physician's horse to a wild posse animal, and I had no doubt that if I allowed her to continue the pace she would drop in her tracks. I did not want to compound the rest of my folly with being left afoot, so I held her there, blowing and dancing and wanting more, and finally she stood still, sides heaving like the blacksmith's bellows.

"Now what, girl?" I said aloud, twisting in the saddle. The shots had come from that general area, but I was no judge of distance. The hills would distort the sound, throwing it this way and that, making out of it an auditory jigsaw puzzle. It was beautiful, emerald-carpeted and wild, but a place to enjoy some other time. I heard a faint sound and turned, looking hard to my left. I was positioned at the top of a crown, with the ravine I had just crossed behind and below me, running off to the left, toward the north. I heard the noise again, sounding like a large animal crashing through brush. Then I caught a glimpse of hide, light-colored, perhaps a thousand yards away, on up the ravine.

I squinted, holding my breath, half rising out of the saddle on the stirrups, watching for more movement. I saw the hide again, like the fleeting glimpse I sometimes got when deer hunting, elusive and too distant for a shot. But I saw, or at least imagined I did, something else that clicked in my head as more than just hide. I saw, for a brief, glinting instant, the metal on a saddle. I pivoted Clara around, the reins sawing her mouth too hard, and we started back down into the ravine, retracing our steps.

The men had hit the ravine, and Blaine had turned north, urging his wounded mount up the easier route provided by the ravine bed.

Knowing that they were close, or at least one of the horses was, I held Clara back, looking for a quiet route rather than a fast one. When we were once more in the bottom of the ravine, I slipped the rifle out of the saddle boot, letting my horse pick her way up the narrow notch between the hills. She made no effort to avoid any but the largest patches of gooseberry, and I ignored the tearing of the thorns against my trouser legs, keeping my eyes glued to the country ahead of me.

And then I found Blaine's stolen horse. It lay on its side in the bed of the ravine, and Clara's ears stood up erect, her eyes big and interested. I reined her in and then saw that the horse was still breathing, shallowly and rapidly. Its head was lying flat, and it made no effort to lift it when we approached. In front of the hip, matted and red, was the wound where the horse had stopped the bullet down in the village. Knowing no better, the horse had plunged on, Blaine astride, until it dropped from loss of blood. And then Bannerman had closed in. For an instant I entertained the notion of putting the animal out of its misery but realized that a shot from my rifle would take away any advantage I might be enjoying. I moved on.

I made another few hundred yards, perhaps halfway to the spot where I had seen the flash of horse before. I was scared. The animal near death that I had just found was not Bannerman's buckskin but, the brief glimpse had shown, with an empty saddle. That meant the score was even . . . both men, if still alive, were on foot, and somewhere in the hills before me, up where the ravine narrowed and then ended in the trees.

I felt like one of those little metal ducks in a circus shooting gallery. Just when every nerve in my body was tensed, and every muscle tight in some mental effort to stop bullets, a gunshot nearly jarred me out of the saddle. It was distant, but the whine of a bullet tearing away into space nearby meant I was the target. Like an idiot, I was perfectly visible, riding right up the center of the ravine, dumb but not happy. I hadn't seen the flash of the gun, and I pulled Clara to a stop. It was the wrong thing to do. A stationary target is easier than a moving one, even at a walk. The next bullet clipped a gooseberry top next to my knee, and the sound of the shot was long an echo by the time I reacted. I dove sideways out of the saddle, and my horse sidestepped away at that unexpected movement, stopping a pace or two away. She eyed me blandly.

With the rifle clutched tightly, I sprinted through the bushes toward the cover of the large timber on the slope, away from the old water cut that had formed the ravine.

I glanced back. Clara was eating with disinterest.

I had a choice. I could either lie there in the trees and wait for something to develop, or press on up the ravine, sticking to the timber and the relative cover provided there. If I was to find Bannerman, lying quiet wouldn't accomplish much. I went to a crouch and threaded my way through the trees. After a few yards I could see that the ravine rose sharply, blending in with another hill that rose like a giant dam at the end of the watercourse, but at the wrong end—the uphill end.

Then I saw the horse. It was Bannerman's buckskin, lying down in the trees near the floor of the ravine. The gelding wasn't moving. I started down toward the animal, then thought better of it. I couldn't do anything for a dead or dying horse, and I would be exposing myself to gunfire from above. I shied away from the ravine, pressing deeper into the timber, making my way upslope. A sharp whistle brought my head around, and there sat John Bannerman, a bemused expression on his face, leaning against the base of a large tree, a tree that grew no more than a yard from the upturned earth of another pine that had toppled years before. Between the living tree and the stump remains, Bannerman had found himself a fortress. He beckoned me toward him with a forefinger, and with a careful scan of the trees uphill from me, I sprinted over to him.

"Damn, I'm glad to see you," I breathed, winded from my run up the hill.

"And I'm glad to see that," Bannerman said, nodding at the rifle in my hands.

"I thought you'd be farther from town than this," I said and looked anxiously up the hill. "Where is he?"

"Up there," the banker said. "I don't think he's got a rifle, so we've got an advantage."

"Advantage! Damn, John, he shot at me when I was at the bottom of this ravine, just past where he left his horse. Anyone that shoots that distance with a revolver and almost hits the mark doesn't need a rifle."

"You saw his horse, then."

"And yours."

Bannerman nodded grimly. "He shot at me a little bit ago and killed the horse. Maybe he wanted to even things up." He pointed across the ravine. "I saw his horse from the other side and crossed over. I think he was waiting for me." He paused.

"You're lucky."

"Maybe. I caught a glimpse of him. Maybe he was moving to a better spot. Robert, he could have taken me any time he wanted. But I saw him and snapped off a quick shot. My horse spooked. He had a clear aim for a few seconds, but then me and the horse were pinwheeling down this slope. What a time for a damn horse to get his legs tangled up. One bullet caught him in the neck, right in front of the saddle."

"If the horse hadn't fallen, you'd be dead."

"Happy thought, Robert. The question is, what now?

I've got four rounds left," Bannerman said, hefting his own Colt revolver. "I hope you've got more than that."

I looked nervously up the hill, feeling naked. "Rifle's loaded, and I've got Kidder's pistol."

"Forty-five?"

"I think it's a forty-four." I reached back and slipped one of the cartridges out of the belt and looked at the back of the casing. "Forty-four."

"Damn."

"You take it. I'm no good with one anyway." I took off the belt and dropped it in Bannerman's lap. For the first time I noticed the odd, uncomfortable position he was holding, his left leg stiff.

"You hurt?"

"Twisted my leg when I went off the horse." He managed a grin. "I'm not as young as I used to be. You mentioned that earlier, I think."

"Can you walk?"

He shook his head. "Won't bear any weight at all."

"What are we going to do, John?" It came out a little more plaintively than I would have liked. Bannerman seemed at ease with the situation, but I wasn't.

"Well," Bannerman mused, looking up the hill carefully, "I figure he's about two hundred yards upslope from here. Just far enough to be dangerous with that damn pistol of his. He doesn't seem to be in much of a hurry. Hasn't shown any signs of wanting to work his way down here to pick us off. You know," and he looked at me, expression bitter, "I think, from what I know of him now, that he's enjoying all this. If he's got any brains at all, he knows we're not lawmen. He shot the only two of them we had."

"Then what's he want to do?"

"My guess would be he'll wait for us to make some stupid mistake, take great pleasure in killing us both, then take your horse and ride out. Your horse is all right?"

"Was when I left her. He shot at me twice, missed both times."

"So you left her down the ravine?"

"Yes."

Bannerman nodded. "Then he knows he's got a mount, if he just waits for us to do . . . whatever. So between you and me, we'd better do it right, whatever it is."

"He won't come to us?"

"I don't think so, not unless he gets desperate. He seems to prefer ambush to outright, frontal attack. His performance so far has indicated that, anyway. He's been perfectly content to harass me from long range, waiting for me to do something."

"And what are we going to do?"

"You have a bad habit of asking that, Robert. I don't know what we're going to do. I just know I want him. I want him more than anything else right now."

"Then let's go get him and get this over with, one way or the other."

"What do you have in mind?"

I looked across the ravine. "I'm going over there. I can make my way around and flank him."

"And he can see you all the way, unless you're a mole."

"The timber's thick enough," I said, hoping it was. "He can't know you're hurt, so . . ."

"Robert, I haven't moved from this spot."

"So?"

"Wouldn't you think that might indicate to him that I'm not exactly mobile anymore?"

"Maybe, but he doesn't know for sure. He sees me, and he has to do something. He'll move, and you can try for a shot."

"With at least a thousand trees in the way."

"For him also." I knelt, staying behind the cover of the big tree. "I'm going across. If you can worm your way up the slope, from tree to tree, maybe you ought to do that."

Bannerman nodded and shifted position painfully. "That may be easier said than done."

"Is anything broken?"

"No, I don't think so."

"Then try. We need to get as close to him as we can."

Bannerman draped the deputy's gun belt over his shoulder and then nodded at me. "All right. Let's try it."

I crouched, then dove downhill, moving as quietly and quickly as I could. The stand of timber was thick, but with little understory growth, so that the trees provided incomplete cover. It would be possible, with careful aim, to send a bullet singing down a fair distance through the trees, but at a moving target, chances of deliberate success would be small. With that encouraging thought in mind, I concentrated on making as rapid progress as I could, weaving and dodging, reaching the ravine and its conspicuous lack of cover without a shot being fired. I stopped, pulling up behind a fat ponderosa, feeling the comfortable four feet of its girth between me and the killer up the hill.

I waited there until my breathing steadied and then took a moment to check the rifle. I hadn't jacked a cartridge into the chamber yet, and did so then, seeing the brass body of the cartridge chuck home in the chamber.

I let the hammer down to the safety notch, took a deep breath, looking out across the gooseberry bushes for the most likely path. I decided on a course that would take me behind the relative cover of a group of four low boulders and, with only a small hesitation, sprinted across, the berry bushes unheeded. I heard the shot and landed on my belly at about the same time, skidding in the gravel of the ravine bottom. I lay stunned for a moment, then dug in and scrambled for the cover of the trees ten yards away. I heard the report of Bannerman's six-gun behind me, four quick shots that told me his own forty-five was now useless. I doubted that any of the slugs made it as far as Blaine, with the trees in the way, but they gave him something to think about, and he held his fire.

My thumb throbbed from being smashed between the ground and the rifle, and then I discovered, on taking my first step at something other than a mad dash, why I had fallen so heavily. The one slug Blaine had sent down ravine toward me, during the fleeting seconds when I was exposed at a distance of at least two hundred yards, had come uncomfortably close. The heel of my right boot was missing, torn off right at the line of the sole by that slug. During all the time I had been in the ravine, with Bannerman, and now making my way up the opposite slope, I had yet to catch sight of Blaine. Wherever he was hidden, he had chosen a perfect spot.

From where I stood then on the opposite side, I could just see Bannerman, and he was crawling on his belly from his spot of protection toward a group of smaller pines. I still could not see Blaine, but I could guess where he was. I leaned against the trunk of a tree, using the bark as a rest for the rifle. Thumbing back the hammer, I tried to judge the distance and fired, the buck of the recoil comforting against my shoulder. I levered the Winchester and fired again, then saw that Bannerman was once more safe behind inches of green wood.

I plunged on up the hill, and I could hear the reports of Bannerman's borrowed revolver, and once the dull moan of a slug that caught a tree partway up the hill, ricocheting off. Blaine wasn't so easily fooled by the pair of amateurs that were trying to assault his position. A veritable hail of bullets whipped through the woods around me, and I yelped, diving for cover, having gained no more than a handful of yards up the hill.

In the next moment it became painfully obvious that Blaine was enjoying the show, sitting somewhere up on the crown of the rise, commanding the entire ravine and hillsides on both sides.

"Run like a rabbit!" came the shout from on high, and then a short burst of laughter, high-pitched bursts of mirth that froze my blood. The laughter was punctuated by four more shots, and I pressed close to the ground, hearing the snap and crack of splintering wood nearby.

"If he doesn't have a rifle, then he's got more than one revolver," I said to the pine needles and thought hopelessly that he wasn't using ammunition like a man running out. When he ran low, he would turn serious, coming down the hill to cut us to pieces and then take Clara and ride off, leaving behind two more corpses to mark his trail.

I squirmed and peered out from behind a stump and caught my breath. Our luck had turned. Confident that I was pinned down, he had adjusted his position to watch Bannerman, and I saw a hint of movement, just the barest flicker of the checkered shirt he had been wearing. I hadn't been shooting anywhere near his position, I realized ruefully, and that was what had prompted his laughter—that and the sight of me scurrying for cover like . . . well, like a rabbit. He was behind a large stump hummock, the roots like a wild woman's hair, twisting and spiraling up in the air after being ripped out of the ground by the large evergreen's fall. He was at the head of the ravine, with thick timber at his back.

Trying not to breath, I slithered the rifle forward, clicking up the second leaf sight for two hundred yards.

Taking my time, I aimed carefully, with just that small patch of cloth for a target, not knowing what part of Blaine's anatomy lay behind it. I gently squeezed the trigger, the boom of the Winchester loud in my ears, the muzzle blast so close to the ground that a small swirl of dust and needles sprayed out, mixing with the smoke to momentarily obscure my target. There was a cry, and I saw a boot and part of a leg shoot out from behind the stump, and then it was withdrawn, leaving no sign of Blaine. He didn't return fire, and I thought for one wild moment that I had actually hit him. But there was no way to tell. I looked across the ravine and caught Bannerman's attention and then tried to tell him by sign language, my antics restricted by trying to remain under cover, that I had at least found the spot where Blaine hid and that I may have hit him.

At the very least, we now knew where he was, and I signaled Bannerman to move forward while I covered him. He did so, and I saw no sign of movement behind the stump high on the hill. After Bannerman had shifted position, gaining perhaps another twenty yards toward Blaine's position, I moved, crabbing sideways, paralleling the ravine and moving up the slope at the same time, hoping that I would be able to circle somewhat behind Blaine's position. There was no movement, no shooting from the outlaw, and my confidence grew.

Bannerman and I continued our advance, alternating, providing cover for each other. When he was no more than fifty yards from the stump fortress of the outlaw, and I no more than sixty, I saw another color that didn't belong, the black of a boot. Just the toe and part of the sole showed, and I spent several long seconds squinting, trying to see more. But that was all. I had a limited number of cartridges remaining in the Winchester. It held twelve, and I racked my brain, trying to remember how many I had fired. I recalled three but wasn't sure. Twelve was all I had started with, thinking then, in my civilian way, that a dozen bullets would be enough, if I had thought about it at all. But I was down to no more than nine, with a killer still sixty yards away. Bannerman had been holding his fire as well, and I guessed that he was thinking the same thoughts. Our protection was running low. Blaine had either been hit or was trying different tactics—and that meant he was no longer content to play games at long range. If he was running low on ammunition, he would make a move to escape. His escape, as I saw it then, could take one of two forms—either on foot, away from us, through the endless timber to who knew where, or through us, to my willing horse down the ravine.

Still seeing the toe of the boot, I rested the rifle again, aiming carefully, putting the spot of boot exactly in the V notch of the back sight, balanced on top of the small, brass front bead like an apple on a fence post. I held my breath and fired. The boot jumped and flopped over. There was no foot in it.

CHAPTER 14

My heart sank somewhere into my gut. I realize that's anatomically impossible, but that's what it felt like. We had been fooled by one of the simplest of ruses. While the birds concerned themselves with the harmless scarecrow in the garden, the clever cat had snuck around behind them and . . . out of reflex I twisted quickly, watching the timber. Was Blaine behind me?

Part of my panic was based on knowledge. A doctor who had treated more than his share of gunshot wounds *knew* what bullets did to flesh. I didn't want any of them in mine.

I had realized the trick of Blaine's, but John Bannerman hadn't. He was crawling forward again, awkward but determined, his bad leg trailing behind him uselessly. Blaine wasn't behind me. He took that opportunity to spring his trap. I saw the smoke from his gun spurt out from a stand of trees behind and to the left of the original gnarled stump where he had first hidden. The shot was still echoing as I watched Bannerman rolling down the incline, revolver flying from his hand.

I sprang up and raced through the timber, crossing the head of the ravine in wild leaps, sprinting for all I was worth, charging toward the stump that now stood between me and the outlaw. Even with those tons of dirt and roots and rocks, Blaine didn't hesitate. He kept to his cover, firing at me with methodical precision, the slugs from his gun blowing debris from the stump, showering me with stinging projectiles. I crouched and then the firing stopped. He had never had a clear shot at me, and he had never bothered to wait for one. I didn't reflect on that until later—much later.

Turning slightly, I looked behind me, taking only enough time to see that John Bannerman was trying to pull himself to a sitting position behind another tree. He was having trouble. I could see the bulk of his shoulders on either side of the tree, and that was even worse. But I was between him and Blaine.

It was a stalemate at close range. The huge stump protected me. The trees on the other side protected Aloysius Blaine. I couldn't risk a shot without exposing myself to his all too accurate gun. The range was so close he couldn't afford to leave his cover to charge my position. I'd hear the first move he made, and his odds, once out in the open, would be slim.

I waited some seconds until my breathing had steadied, then stuck the barrel of the Winchester through a tangle of roots, keeping everything but my hand under cover. I fired in the general direction I knew Blaine to be. My shot was followed almost instantly by a savage barrage of answering fire, so close I imagined I could feel the waves of heat coming from the outlaw's revolver. The air was full of junk from the stump, and I cringed down, even though I was perfectly safe—as long as both of us held position.

I glanced downhill again and saw two hands on either side of the pine as John Bannerman fought to pull himself to his feet. He peered out from behind the tree, then shuffled into view. I shook my head wildly at him, and he stopped. He held Kidder's revolver up, ready for any target. But he was swaying on his feet. I shook my head again, levered, and fired the Winchester. That brought on another fury of fire from Blaine, five rounds this time, accompanied by an equally savage barrage of cursing.

The shooting stopped finally but not the wild yelling of a man possessed.

"There, you sons a bitches," Blaine screamed, "Take what you come for!" There was a dull thud against the stump, and a Colt revolver pinwheeled over and bounced down the hill. I stared at it uncomprehendingly. The man had run out of ammunition and in a rage had even thrown his gun at the stump where his enemy hid.

"I say come and get me, you yella-bellied bastards!" Blaine screamed again, his voice clearer—as if he had stepped out from behind his cover. I hesitated, then bent down, finding a spot low on the stump mass where I could see through with minimal risk and still manage a shot. Aloysius Blaine was standing clear, one boot on, the other off, hands at his sides. I saw no weapon.

Keeping him in view, I slowly came out from behind the huge stump, stepping out past the widespread, rotting roots. I held the rifle cocked and high, finger tense on the trigger.

"Well, now, if it ain't the doctor," he said and, damn him, grinned and then laughed. He made no attempt to move, gambling then that I wouldn't gun him down where he stood.

"Put your hands over your head," I said. I motioned with the rifle, its barrel steady.

He smiled again, eyes fixed on me. "Don't think I will," he said quietly. We stood no more than ten yards apart, alone on the hill.

I jerked the rifle toward him, threatening. "I'll shoot."

"Don't think you will," he said calmly. I remembered the string of curses, the hysterically thrown revolver. This man was far from the maniac out of control, and I knew then I had walked into another trap—Blaine's ultimate gamble that face to face, man to man, I would not be able to pull the trigger.

"Didn't know until just a bit ago that it was you comin' up the hill," he said, as if carrying on a conversation with a good friend. "I wouldn't have made you work so hard at it." He chuckled again and took a casual step toward me. My finger went white on the trigger.

"You make another move and I'll drop you," I said.

"If you was about to shoot me, you woulda done it at the right time," he said, smiling again but with no good will behind that smile. For no reason that made any sense, it was those words that brought Bernie Kidder to mind, and his words when we last saw each other in Colby.

"You see him, you shoot him," Kidder had said, adding, "don't be a damn fool."

Aloysius Blaine had had two revolvers. As Kidder's words ran through my head, his hand reached behind him, not fast, but almost casually, and came out with the six-gun. I didn't act out of reflex but stood like an idiot, watching that handgun sweep up, its large bore coming up at the same time Blaine's thumb clicked back the hammer. At that range, I could even see the gray, deadly cones of lead in the cylinders, rotating up, the one that would kill me coming under the spot where the hammer would fall.

Blaine's calm premeditated act froze me in my tracks. He knew he had won, and he smiled again.

"Thanks for the use of your horse," he said. It is incredibly hard for any human being to speak and squeeze the trigger of a gun at the same time. There was that lag while he spoke, and it was enough. That one sentence, void of all real emotion or compunction, kicked my mind hard—so hard that I jerked the trigger of the Winchester, a bare fraction of a second before Blaine pulled the trigger of his Colt. My lack of marksmanship, even at that range, saved my life. The bullet hit him hard in the left shoulder, shattering the joint and spinning him like a top to his left, so that the bullet from his own gun slapped harmlessly past my ear.

He hit the ground hard, the revolver flying from his grip to land five feet away. His eyes bugged, and he gasped, coming to his knees, facing away from me. With his right hand clutching the jagged wound, he turned and looked at me, surprised.

"You did it," he said, as if he was amazed, and he shook his head. He put his good arm down, supporting himself, holding his left arm close to his body, and began to crawl toward where the Colt lay in the needles.

Seeing him crawling toward the gun, my mind seemed clear since the first time on the hill. I could have beaten him to it easily, kicked it off into the woods, or taken it up and stuck it in my belt.

But I remembered the look on John Bannerman's face as he leaned, wounded, against the tree down the hill. And I remembered Bernie Kidder, and the marshal, and the old doctor—even the woman in Bayard. Add to that four counts from rustling sick cattle and then selling them to innocent people. The names and faces of those people filed through my mind like a litany, and I levered the Winchester.

Blaine heard the sound and glanced at me, that insanely calm smile returning to his lips, his blood running down into the pine needles.

He reached for the Colt, squatted back, and picked it up, awkward from the pain and the shock.

"Don't be a goddamned fool," Deputy Bernie Kidder said again somewhere in my skull. I aimed the Winchester carefully and then pulled the trigger.

finally across the meadow, coming out on the tree-guarded ridge above Colby. The sun was hot, almost directly overhead. We rested there for a while, Bannerman holding on to the saddle horn with a grip that turned his knuckles as white as his face.

"Didn't know if I'd ever see that sight again," he said. We started down the last hill, past the mines and toward the village. There was no one working the mines, and I realized with a start that it was Sunday—a brilliantly clear, warm Sunday.

"How's the deputy?" Bannerman asked.

"He'll be all right," I said. "He's going to lose some movement of his right arm. I don't know if he'll be able to keep his job or not."

"I wonder . . ." and Bannerman winced as the sway of Clara's back twisted his hip, "I wonder if after all this he's just a little annoyed at us for doing his job."

"I don't think so," I answered and then dug into my shirt pocket and fished out the badge. "It was all legal."

Bannerman saw the star. "Well, I'll be damned," he said. "So now you're a lawman!"

"Small chance of that. No chance, as a matter of fact. As soon as we get down this hill, Bernie gets it back, for good."

"He's going to be annoyed."

"No, I don't think so."

"I do. His six-gun is still up there on the hill."

"But you had it!"

"I did," Bannerman said ruefully. "I put it to one side while you were butchering my leg. I forgot to pick it up."

"He'll be annoyed. That's about a month's pay."

"He's lucky he's alive to be annoyed. I'll buy him another one." I nodded and we went on in silence, me

CHAPTER 15

"He's dead?"

"Yes," I said and laid the rifle down beside John Bannerman.

"Then it's over."

"I hope so." I used my pocketknife to cut some of the trouser material away and examined the wound. The bullet had hit Bannerman in his already bad leg, high in the thigh, angling down through the heavy muscle. It had cut a bloody furrow almost to his kneecap.

"I seem to have it in for that leg," he said and grimaced.

"It's not as bad as it looks."

"We going to take Blaine back in?"

I shook my head. "Clara will carry you, and I'll walk. I don't see any point in taking him in," I said bitterly. I looked at the wound again. "Well, you're not bleeding to death. Relax while I go get the horse and my bag." The walk down seemed shorter, and I found my horse, browsing as if nothing had happened. In another half hour I had Bannerman's leg bandaged and him in the saddle. A twisted hip makes a Western saddle an instrument of torture, and the banker's face was white. I gave him some morphine and that seemed to help, except he sat so loosely that I was afraid he would flop out of the saddle, doing even more damage. We picked our way carefully out of the ravine, up through the hills, and trudging along beside Clara's gurgling gut as her head nodded sleepily.

"What are you going to do when we get back to Cooperville, John?"

He sighed. "See if my bank's still in one piece, I guess. Try to pick up where I left off. There's some problems need solving in town, Robert. That will keep me busy."

"You're going to stay?"

He looked down at me quizzically. "Well, of course. What made you think otherwise?"

I shrugged. "Just wondered."

"It's my home. Wouldn't accomplish anything by pulling up stakes." He looked on ahead. "We've got company."

Several horsemen were riding slowly up the hill toward us, and I recognized two or three of them from the night previous. They met us a hundred yards from the edge of the village, and they were heavily armed, faces grim. They had evidently taken their own sweet time coming to a decision to help.

"What happened?" one of them asked when they drew up to us.

"Blaine's dead," I said, feeling no exhilaration at being able to say that. The horsemen looked relieved, and they escorted us back into Colby, forming a respectful circle around us. No one thought to offer me a mount, but then a hundred yards didn't seem like much after climbing mountains on one's belly and dodging bullets.

CHAPTER 16

It was early October. Fall had come fast and hard to Cooperville, the cottonwoods that ringed the village turning to gold in a quick burst, then browning and pelting the town with crisp old paper. The air had a bite, and the wind was insistent, blowing up the main street, pushing the leaves and the dust ahead of it in small, swirling clouds.

I ate dinner at the Branding Iron, enjoying a lamb stew that I thought was a genuine marvel of flavor, taking several servings from Marion as she watched, face set sternly. Their business was almost normal, I thought, and Tom had made a full recovery, left only with the seven scars that he would carry for the rest of his life.

"Of course you'll have dessert," she said, and I couldn't remember even mentioning the subject. I was uncomfortably tight in the belt already.

"Would coffee be all right?" I asked. "I don't have room for anything else."

"Course you have," she said severely. "I didn't bake pie all day to watch it sit on the shelf."

There was no arguing with the woman. She brought the raspberry pie, and I sighed and set to work. I was almost finished when she brought the coffee, then promptly retreated for a second cup. John Bannerman, his limp only barely discernible, entered the Branding

Iron and sat down opposite me at the small table, elbows on the checkered cloth.

"How's the food?" he said and then leaned back as Marion set the cup in front of him and poured the strong coffee for him. "Thank you, dear lady," Bannerman said and smiled at her. She favored him with a smile in return.

"The food is too much," I said and shoved the remains of the pie toward him. "Want to finish that?"

Bannerman held up his hands, shaking his head.

"I need your advice," he said, leaning his chin in his hands.

"On what?"

"I got a letter today."

"Oh?"

"Uh-huh. From Bernie Kidder."

I looked up in surprise. "Really?"

Bannerman nodded. "He's hunting a job."

I set my fork down and took a sip of the scalding coffee. "A job?"

"Yes. He says he has almost full use of his arm, but Max Edmunds has kept him pretty restricted. From what he says, he hasn't been out of the office since our return. Been doing paperwork, cleaning guns, and generally, if I read between the lines, going stir-crazy."

"What kind of a job does he want?"

"Town marshal."

"You're serious?"

"Indeed I am."

"What about McCuskar?"

Bannerman hesitated, then cleared his throat. "We had a quick meeting last night. Seems he got so drunk in the Apple Core that two patrons had to carry him back home. We can't have that, Robert."

"I tried to tell you that some months ago."

"I know you did. I may move like molasses, but at least I moved. We had a meeting last night and set some records for brevity. We fired Mr. McCuskar."

"I'm glad to hear that. And you got the letter from Kidder this morning?"

Bannerman nodded. "Fortuitous, wouldn't you say?"

There was something in the tone of his voice that made me wonder what cards were up his sleeve. He saw my expression and chuckled. "Well, to tell the truth, I wrote Mr. Kidder myself, more than a week ago, suggesting."

"Ah," I said, nodding. "Then the matter is over and done with. What advice do you want from me?"

"Well, there's the matter of his arm," Bannerman said, folding his hands around the coffee cup. "I told him in that letter that the job would be, ah, contingent on your approval of his general health and ability to do the job."

"I see. I wouldn't think being a town marshal is quite as demanding as being a deputy for Max Edmunds."

"You'll look at him, then? He'll be here at the end of the week. Sounded eager."

"Of course. But I can tell you right now you've made a good choice. Bernie Kidder is ten times the lawman Vince McCuskar ever thought of being."

"We agree, then. You know, I thought first of you."

"Of me?"

"Yes. I contemplated, seriously, I might add, offering you the job."

"Don't be ridiculous."

"Yes," Bannerman said. "You've said that before." He

laughed and sipped the coffee. "Kidder said it would be a pleasure working in a town where he knew the town fathers and knew he had their support. He mentioned me by name, and he mentioned you. I thought you'd appreciate knowing, at your early stage in life, that you're already a 'town father.' "

I started to make some caustic reply, then thought better of it. John Bannerman was right. It felt good.

"I'd like to build an infirmary," I said suddenly, not knowing precisely what brought it to mind.

"That's commendable."

"I don't have the money."

Bannerman threw back his head and roared and slapped the table. "Then let's go to my office and talk about it," he said, still shaking with laughter.

"It's somewhat late," I said. It was. Already dark outside, the wind with a bite to it that cut through the clothing.

"It's never that late, Robert my boy. I'll have you so deeply in debt that this town will be virtually guaranteed a physician for decades to come." He rubbed his hands in mock glee. We walked out into the fall air together, both of us feeling so alive with plans that we worked far into the night. It was good to be home.

Steven Havill has worked as a reporter, a photographer, and an editor in New York and in New Mexico, where he now lives. His first novel, *The Killer,* was published as a Double D Western in 1981.